DATE DUE			
MAR 7 0			
APR 12 '01			
MAY 1 7 01			
MY 27 '03			
JY 27 '03			
8-3-04			
10-25-04			
JUN 29 20			
JL 27 20			

01/01

JACKSON COUNTY
Library Services

HEADQUARTERS
413 West Main Street
Medford, Oregon 97501

THE SPLENDID VISTA

*Also by Esther Loewen Vogt
in Large Print:*

Song of the Prairie
Edge of Dawn
The Flame & The Fury

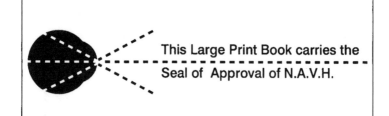

This Large Print Book carries the
Seal of Approval of N.A.V.H.

The Splendid Vista

Esther Loewen Vogt

Thorndike Press • Thorndike, Maine

Thorndike Press Large Print Christian Fiction Series.

The text of this Large Print edition is unabridged.
Other aspects of the book may vary from the original edition.

Set in 16 pt. Plantin by PerfecType.

Library of Congress Cataloging-in-Publication Data

Vogt, Esther Loewen.
  The splendid vista / Esther Loewen Vogt.
    p. cm.
  ISBN 0-7862-2799-0 (lg. print : hc : alk. paper)
    1. United States — History — Civil War, 1861–1865 —
Fiction. 2. Antietam, Battle of, Md., 1862 — Fiction.
3. Church of the Brethren — Fiction. 4. Physicians —
Fiction. 5. Nurses — Fiction. 6. Large type books. I. Title.
PS3572.O3 S6 2000
  813′.54—dc21   00-055183

To
Celeta Parker,
my good friend and fellow author,
who encouraged me,
steered, and helped me
in Civil War research.

AUTHOR'S NOTE

For readers such as myself, who like to have the fact and fiction sorted out, I offer the following:

The Battle of Antietam really took place on September 17, 1862, near Sharpsburg, Maryland. Often referred to as "the bloodiest day" of the Civil War, casualties were heavier than in any known war in history in one day of fighting. Nearly 23,000 soldiers were wounded or killed in that one day. All battle incidents in this novel are factual, including the part the little Dunker Church played in the war. Although badly battered, it served as a hospital, along with many homes and farm buildings. The German Baptist Brethren, members of a plain sect, were affluent farmers with names such as Poffenberger, Mumma, Miller, Hoffman, and Geeting. In fact, Samuel Mumma was the presiding elder of the congregation, often referred to as the "Mumma Church."

The Manor Church some seven miles north was considered the "mother church."

According to *Doctors in Blue* by George W. Adams, medical procedures as they appear in the story are accurate. Sterilizing surgical instruments was not practiced until shortly after the war, and amputations were common. Clara Barton really served as a nurse at this battle in the famous Miller cornfield, according to her diary. She also removed a bullet from a wounded soldier. Espousing pacifism, but favoring the Union side, the German Baptist Brethren helped nurse both Rebel and Yankee wounded in their homes. All generals and Chaplain George Bullen, Drs. Dunn, Biggs, and Letterman were real.

I have pored through volumes on the Civil War, especially on the Antietam Battle. I have read pamphlets on the Mumma Church, including one by Oliver Reilly, which was written several years after the war and contains interviews of people who saw firsthand what went on that bloody day.

The novel, however, is a work of fiction. Names and characters are either the product of my imagination, or if real, are based on fact and used fictitiously.

— Esther Loewen Vogt
Hillsboro, Kansas

The *Splendid* *Vista*

There is neither Jew nor Greek, slave nor free, male nor female, for you are all one in Christ Jesus.

Galatians 3:28, NIV.

1

The rains had been copious that summer of 1861 in Washington County, Maryland. On this Saturday morning the bright August sun already blazed in the clear blue sky, and Sharpsburg's main street bustled with the clatter of wagons, creak of carts, and the hollow thud of horses' hooves. The day promised to be warm, for only a mild breeze fanned the humid air.

Kirsten Weber drew her horse Polly to a stop before Smith's General Store, and slid from the saddle, tying the reins loosely to the hitching rail. Smoothing her dark gray skirt, she picked up the basket of eggs from the pommel carefully and crossed the threshold of the red brick store. It was a jumbled, pleasant place that smelled of oiled floorboards, new cloth and leather, and fresh ground coffee. Its one dusty window with a worn, dark green blind hanging drunkenly across it, looked out on the narrow, rutted street beyond.

Carefully setting the basket of eggs on the rough wooden counter, Kirsten waited. Elias Smith was busily weighing out dried beans from the sack behind him for a customer. His balding gray head and pepper-and-salt mustache accented his lined face.

"Will that be all, Thomas?" he asked as he tied the brown paper sack with a stout piece of string.

"All for now, Elias. Martha needs the beans to soak for tomorrow's dinner. Any news from the war front?" Thomas Geeting drew out his wallet, smoothed out a few crumpled bills, and laid them on the counter.

"Bull Run, you know. Too bad. Seems the president has handed the reins over to General McClellan since McDowell got beat. There ain't much else new that I've heard."

Thomas Geeting passed a hand over his grizzled, bearded face. "McDowell started out grand enough. A brilliant procession trailed by congressmen and fine ladies in carriages rode proudly out of Washington toward Manassas. But they retreated right quick when the Union soldiers come back with their tails between their legs."

Kirsten drew a sharp breath. She was in no mood to listen to depressing war talk, for she wanted to hurry home with her purchases and cook dinner for her family. Shoving her basket of eggs toward the proprieter, she moistened her dry lips.

"I'd like — "

"McClellan'll do a good job and wipe up the whole mess, if he's in charge," Elias went on, counting out change carefully. "President Lincoln's got lots of faith in Little Mac."

"I don't know, but I sure hope you're right. Well, I'd better get on home with these beans," Geeting said, picking up his sack of purchases. Turning, he tipped his broad-brimmed black hat as he noticed Kirsten standing beside him at the counter. "Good morning, Sister Weber," he added, then left.

Kirsten watched him go, aware of neat patches on his blue trousers. The Geetings were less affluent than most of the Dunker Church folk.

Pulling out her short list, she handed it to the proprieter, and wandered around the store while waiting for her order to be filled. The musky aroma of drying bean pods and barrel of pickle brine seemed to permeate the rest of the shop, and she sniffed disdainfully. Catching sight of herself in the mirror hanging crookedly on the rear door, she paused briefly. Do I look so dusty and disheveled from my ride? she thought. Luckily she was tall enough not to stretch her slim figure for a glimpse in the mirror.

Pushing back her black bonnet, she re-arranged the coils of rich brown hair pinned firmly on the nape of her shapely neck. A few stray tendrils threatened to escape from the tortoise-shell pins and she tacked them snugly behind her ears. Her delicately carved cheeks, her straight Weber nose, determined chin, and wide frank mouth looked fair — almost pretty. Then she whirled away. The typical dark, long sleeves, the high neckline of her dress, and black bonnet identified her as a member of the "Dunker Church," as the German Baptist Brethren were called. Vanity was not one of their attributes.

With a small sigh she hurried back to the counter. Elias Smith had filled her order and was adding the sums on a thick gray tablet with a stubby lead pencil.

"You had enough eggs to cover the cost of your purchases, and forty-seven cents left over," he said, counting out the money in her palm. "How is your father? Still busy with the work of the church?"

Kirsten nodded. "He's been elected elder,

you know. His job is to make sure supplies for the needy are delivered." She picked up her parcels and started for the door. "Do you — do you think the war will be over soon? We're so near the Potomac River, and when the fighting's going on in the state of Virginia right west of us — "

"Don't worry, Miss. Now that McClellan's in charge of Union forces, he's sure to wind things up in a hurry."

Kirsten smiled and hurried out to her horse. She hoped he was right. The talk of war had lain like a shadow over their lives for months. If only it were over soon. She remembered her father had asked her to stop for mail. The post office was kept in the Kuhn house near the Big Spring. It was on her way out of town.

Inside the post office she clutched the two church publications addressed to her father that Mr. Kuhn had handed her, and started for the door when she heard a familiar giggle.

"Kirsten! How were you able to break away from all your work so early on a Saturday morning?" Allie Mumma's lilting voice greeted her. The bubbly, vivacious face beamed at her from its traditional black bonnet.

"Well, Lelo's old enough. It's time she carries some of the load."

15

The short, blond figure took a few mincing steps backward. 'Yes, it's high time you groomed your sisters to look after the household. The way David Poffenberger's been eyeing you at Meeting — "

"I'm not ready to think of marrying for a long time," Kirsten snapped. "Since Mama died, it's been my duty to look after the family."

"But you can't do that forever," Allie said frowning. "One of these days you'll fall in love and leave your father's household. Remember — you're nineteen years old. Don't be too dedicated!"

"I know that, Allie. But what would Papa do without me? Peter's just seventeen, and Lelo's not quite sixteen. And the two younger ones — "

"Train Lelo so when the times comes, you won't feel obligated to stay home."

Kirsten frowned. It wouldn't be easy to train the dreamy-eyed, flighty Lieselotte. "Well, the time hasn't come, and I haven't fallen in love, so there's no need to worry. Besides, I'm sure David Poffenberger understands my position. As long as Papa and the family need me — "

"*Ach,* even the Lord wouldn't expect you to sacrifice yourself for your family, Kirsten," Allie flung out as she hurried out the door.

16

With a heavy sigh, Kirsten went out to her horse and settled herself in the saddle. Allie was so incurably romantic that she'd tried to shove every available girl she knew into some man's arms. Well, Kirsten Weber wasn't ready for love. Of that she was sure.

Polly cantered lazily along the hot, dusty street that meandered out of Sharpsburg to the north. The hilly terrain of Washington County that scooped the Maryland countryside into cups and ravines stretched out endlessly. The road wound nearly a mile west of the Hagerstown turnpike, and the Weber farm lay hidden around the bend of a hill some two or three miles farther northwest. The dirt road crept between split rail fences, sifting with wisps of dust as she rode along.

A mile west ahead lay the West Woods, to the east of the road along which she cantered. On its other side, just a mile north of town, sat the simple little whitewashed Dunker Church beside the Hagerstown pike. The woods of tall walnut trees stood like sentinels in the quiet August morning, patterning the grass with a mosaic of sunshine and shadow.

Kirsten had told nine-year-old Heidi to sweep the house and hang the goose feather pillows out to air. Lelo surely would have set

17

the pan of salt-rising bread for baking. Saturdays were really too busy for her to waste riding into town, but she had run out of brown sugar for the sweet buns, and dried fruit to stew for Sunday dinner, plus a few other items. Besides, it wasn't often she rode into Sharpsburg. If her father or Peter hadn't been haying, they might have offered to go on her errand.

Immersed in her musing, Kirsten was unaware of the fox that leaped from the woods until it bolted in front of Polly. The horse whinnied, reared suddenly, and sent Kirsten flying from the saddle. She landed with a thud on the soft grass beside the road with a sharp cry, one leg doubled under her. She tried to straighten it, but the pain was too sharp. With dismay she saw Polly trot down the road toward home.

Bewildered, Kirsten sank back on the grass. Her black bonnet had been torn from her head in the fall and flung several feet away, tumbling her brown hair from its pins and drooping it over her shoulders.

Swallowing her despair, she tried once more to free her foot, groaning with the effort. Fighting tears as she struggled to move, the pain drove her down again.

"Please lie back, Miss," a voice spoke beside her. Startled, Kirsten looked up. A tall

18

young man had dropped to his knees and gently lifted her so that the painful leg slid free. He had tossed his felt hat on the grass; now he slipped off her boot carefully. Luckily she had worn only footlets in her boots instead of the usual black stockings.

A wave of embarrassment swept over her when she felt the stranger's hands moving expertly over her bare ankle. She winced as he probed and tested, his capable fingers touching the bruised area He looked to be about twenty-five years old, with a thatch of dark brown hair that fell back in waves from the side part. His eyes were the deep blue of a midsummer sky. A neatly trimmed mustache lent grace to his ruddy face, and a mild frown seemed to track across his forehead between the eyes, giving him a slightly disapproving look. His dark blue coat was cut in the fashionable style of the day, and the tight-fitting fawn colored trousers were tucked neatly into polished black boots. Most of all, she noticed his strong slender fingers that moved expertly over her leg.

Reaching into his side pocket, he drew out a fine white handkerchief. "It's your ankle, Miss. You've had a bad sprain. I'll wrap it tightly and you'll be all right. But you'd best stay off your feet for a few days — maybe a week at least."

"How — " She eyed him with a puzzled frown. "How do you know — "

"My name's Wilshire Patten and I'm a medical student, studying in Georgetown University School of Medicine in Washington. I'm on my way home to Hagerstown for a few weeks' leave. Please just call me Wil."

"Mister — Doctor Wil," Kirsten stammered, "I don't — know how to thank you enough. But as for staying off my feet — "

"Where do you live?" he cut in. "I saw your horse go flying over yonder — " He pointed down the road that disappeared around the bend of the hill.

"That was Polly." Kirsten nodded, then winced with pain again. "Our farm is hidden beyond that hill over there. My family will worry when Polly comes home without me."

"I'll take you home," Wil Patten said, springing back on his heels in one graceful movement, "if you'll tell me who you are," he added, his blue eyes alive with interest that made the pucker above his forehead disappear.

She bit her lower lip. "My name is Kirsten Weber, and I'm the — the head of the family," she said a bit stiffly.

He eyed her curiously. "The head of a family? You have children?"

20

"Oh. . . ." She smiled wanly, trying to mask her pain. "Forgive me for being so — dense. I — we are five siblings and we do have a father. Our mother is — dead."

"I'm sorry to hear that. I know what it means to lose a parent." He glanced around and spied the black bonnet and picked it up and brushed it off carefully. "This yours?"

"Yes." She nodded, embarrassed, fumbling with the dark coils of her hair that sagged over her back. "I'm — sorry. My hair. . . ." She pushed the escaping ringlets back behind her ears.

"Never mind. It's beautiful!" He started to reach for her hair, then drew back. "You are of the German Baptist Brethren?"

"Yes. We're sometimes called Dunkers. I was baptized upon the confession of my faith in the Antietam Creek when I was fourteen."

"Oh." He toyed awkwardly with her bonnet, then laid it gently on her lap. "Well, I'll get Beecher — that's my stallion. You see, I was riding through the woods when I must've startled the fox that spooked your horse, and sent you sailing through the air. I stopped as quickly as I could." He picked up his hat and gave a low whistle. A splendid black horse trotted gracefully from the woods toward them. He took the reins and patted the smooth glossy mane, speaking to the animal in low, comforting tones.

Kirsten had managed to scoop her long hair back into its coil and jammed the bonnet on her head. She blushed at the thought of "sailing through the air." How undignified she must have looked to this polished young doctor!

He stood watching her, then knelt beside her again. "Ready? Shall I lift you on Beecher's back?"

She nodded shyly, and he picked her up gently and set her on the horse. She felt a tingle as his hands slid around her slender waist. It was a new feeling — something she had never experienced before. Silly, she scolded herself fiercely — why must I feel a thrill at the first strange man who touches me?

"Comfortable?" he asked solicitiously, positioning her injured foot carefully on the other side of the stallion.

Kirsten nodded again. He was such a kind young man and so polite. Perhaps that's why her heart raced so madly.

As he led the horse gently down the road, he turned his head toward her. "I noticed the church across the woods on the Hagerstown pike. Is that where you worship?"

"Yes," she said, her heart slowing down a

little. "My father is an elder. He's very busy with the charitable work of the church these days."

"Doesn't a pretty girl like you find the 'plain folk' a bit — boring?" he asked whimsically.

The horse's trot was gentle and the pain in her ankle made Kirsten wince, but she jerked her head at his words.

"Boring?" she flared. "Never. My Christ gives me inner strength, inner life. You don't understand, do you?"

"Perhaps not. I'm sorry for upsetting you, but it's not often that I find such a beautiful girl — "

"Please don't say any more," she cut in brusquely, jutting out her chin stubbornly. "I'm sorry to bother you like this." Her voice was cold.

He laughed and his laughter sounded like deep-toned bells. "I guess I must seem very pompous and brash, and I'm sorry if I've come across to you as a boor. But I'm glad I happened along when I did. With my medical training — "

"Yes, yes, of course," she interrupted, her features softening, "and I'm very grateful." She paused and looked beyond the rise of the hill. In the far, gray distance she saw the shimmer of the Potomac, with green tilled fields below where her father and brother Peter were raking the last of the hay. "Do you think the war will be over soon?" she added, recalling the gossip she'd heard in the store earlier.

"I'm afraid the Union forces are in for a siege," he said gravely. "Of course, if McClellan is too cautious — as he's prone to be — this can well happen. But I still have nearly seven months of study, including surgery, in school. Surely by then it will all be over. Being a border state, Maryland is mostly pro-Union, you know, although there are some Rebels. But it may not touch us at all."

"You're going to be a surgeon?" Kirsten asked, with sudden interest in the polite young man.

"Yes. Someday I hope to set up a medical practice in the capital — if I'm lucky. If war continues, I'll serve my country in some Union hospital, no doubt."

Overhead, the sun now seeped with a muted light through a thin layer of white clouds, and a brooding danger, as gray and dark as a winter storm, seemed to have crept over the countryside at the mention of the war. Kirsten shivered in the warm morning — a feeling she couldn't shake.

War was wrong. The Bible said that

Christians were to love their enemies. That was Christ's command. But if it came here, how would she react? And what would it do to this young man's dream of being a doctor?

"Do you feel it's wrong to own another man — a slave?" she asked.

"Oh, yes!" His voice rang with conviction. "I believe most of us Marylanders do, and I believe slaves should be freed."

As the horse had reached the bend and turned into the lane of the Weber farm, the low painted barns and tall, imposing whitewashed brick house burst into view. Polly stood at the barnyard gate, nickering and waiting to be led into her stall. Kirsten's brother Andrew, his tousled sandy head bare, was already heading for the barn.

"Kirsten?" he called out, his voice shrill and sharp. "Kirsten, where are you?"

The eleven-year-old must be worried, Kirsten thought. "Here I am, Andrew," she replied as the stallion reached the gate. "Polly was frightened and threw me. But Doctor — Doctor Wilshire Patten found me and brought me home. Wasn't that good of him?"

Andrew's keen blue eyes grew wide and his brow furrowed at her bandaged ankle. "You're hurt, Kirsten!"

"I'll be all right. That is, if Dr. Patten knows what he's doing."

Wil laughed again. "You may be sure of that, Andrew." He stopped before the house and helped Kirsten to the ground. Andrew ran ahead and opened the neatly painted picket gate. Faded maroon hollyhocks still nodded over the palings. Kirsten limped as the young medical student helped her up the brick path to the porch, his arm tucked snugly around her waist.

She paused with her hand on the knob of the front door. "I'll be fine now, Dr. Patten — Wil. Thanks — very much." She pulled away from him and reached out her hand. He took it between both of his and held it until she jerked it away. She was right. He was brash as well as polite.

Bowing a little, he looked into her gray eyes. "Kirsten — in two weeks I'll head back down the pike for Washington. May I stop back and see you — to check on your ankle?" he added tactfully.

A shower of sparks shot through her and she shook herself to clear them away, feeling red color seep into her cheeks. Did she want to see this brash young doctor again? Something told her it was inevitable, whether she wanted it consciously or not.

"I — " she whispered, steadying herself against the door. "If the Lord wills." Her words were low.

With that, she slammed the door and limped into the house.

2

The days ran slowly — heavy and golden like honey — and daily Kirsten felt strength pour into her injured ankle. The family had rallied around her, Lieselotte and Heidi quite capably although somewhat diffidently carrying out her orders in the house. Peter, thin and dark, worked silently beside their tall, sparsely built, brown-bearded father in the hayfields, while wiry Andrew managed the farmyard chores.

Kirsten drew a deep breath of satisfaction today. Perhaps she wasn't as indispensable as she had thought. Yet it bothered her a little. It was good to be needed, although the enforced rest had been welcome. Now she felt completely recovered.

She couldn't stifle thoughts of the tall young doctor and wondered if he would stop by on his way to Washington as he had promised. Then she shook off the idea

People of his calibre — polished, wealthy, educated — soon forgot rashly made promises to obscure girls of a plain sect. It was best she ignored his brash question about seeing her again. Of course, he meant medically, to check her ankle.

Tomorrow was Sunday and the family would attend worship services in the little white Dunker church as usual. Kirsten knew it was not a "love feast" Sunday that meant an all-day meeting. At this gathering after a half hour of unaccompanied singing, one of the Brethren would rise to his feet and testify of the love and power of God. After the sermon, in commemoration of the Last Supper, one of the elders would gird himself with a towel around his waist and wash and dry the feet of the man next to him. This rite would be performed by each member of the congregation, followed by a handshake — the "right hand of fellowship," the "holy kiss," and a communion meal of lamb stew, again celebrating the Last Supper. The services usually ended with a closing hymn and prayer.

Now that Albert Weber had been elected elder, he was one of the men who presided over Sunday services, for the church had no paid pastor like the Lutherans in Sharpsburg.

Kirsten's heart warmed with love for the Brethren and the oneness of fellowship and closeness of communion among its members. *I must keep in mind,* she reminded herself firmly, *that someone like Wilshire Patten would never fit into a group with the spiritual dedication of our German Baptist Brethren.*

Now she busied herself in the substantial, comfortable kitchen tacked onto the rear of the large brick farmhouse. A chimney jutting out from the huge fireplace as though proud of big fires and big dinners, stood at the east end, and a heavy black crane swung from its north end. A roomy oven with a heavy top which baked delectable cakes and crusty biscuits and breads took up the south wall.

The room had no ceiling. The blackened rafters and high shadowy spaces contrasted with the whitewashed walls and scrubbed puncheon floor. At whitewashing time — as much a sign of springtime as the leafing of walnuts and elms — all buildings were whitewashed. The kitchen inside and out was a glistening sugary white, like a huge iced cake. The biscuit block was a square, marble slab mounted on a high frame with a wooden cover that was removed when biscuits or bread dough was pounded or kneaded on the smooth surface. Today

Kirsten's three loaves of wheat bread dough were rising, smoothly oiled, in the pans.

Heidi bounced into the kitchen, her bare feet plopping on the wooden floor, waving her dustcloth.

"Oh, Kirsten, I'm glad you're back on the job," she said, swishing the cloth airily. "I'm tired of being Lelo's slave and at her beck and call every second."

"You were never your sister's slave," Kirsten chided gently, whacking slabs of meat into the heavy iron skillet to brown for the noon meal. "You know we don't hold with slavery."

"Well, sometimes it seemed that way. Andrew and I haven't had time for play in almost two weeks."

Kirsten turned and patted her young sister's fat blond braids. "Tell you what, Heidi. After you've trimmed the lamps and pressed your best gray poplin for tomorrow, and made sure you have memorized your Scriptures, you and Andrew may play in the South Woods until suppertime. I guess my being laid up has been rather hard on you."

Lelo sauntered dreamily into the kitchen at that moment, sloshing a pail of water she had brought from the spring that gurgled cool and sweet from the cave below the hill.

"Oh, Kirsten," she sang out. "It's a beautiful morning. Life is wonderful and I hope it never changes. It's a great day for mooning. . . ."

"Not until your work is done, Lelo," Kirsten cut in tersely. "Better leave the moon for now. It's time to set the dinner table. Papa and Peter will be in from the fields soon.

The clatter of flatware and the slam of crockery dishes on the red-checked tablecloth intermingled with the hissing sounds of frying meat and sputtering of potatoes on the hearth. The farmhouse was filled with the aroma of good cooking and bustle of work, and Kirsten breathed a prayer of thanks that she was a part of the family's work force again.

A few minutes later the family sat down to eat. After bowing his head for table grace, Albert Weber speared a large piece of meat.

"Tomorrow we begin plans for our newest charity project in church," he said. "I will meet with my committee after dinner, so it's important that we hurry home after the services."

"Just so Kirsten whomps up a big meal," Andrew said, wolfing down a piece of cornbread soaked with molasses. "It's good to eat her cooking again. I'll be on my way home the minute Elder Mumma says 'amen.'"

"This is nothing to josh about, Andrew," Papa said sternly. "I just wanted to remind you — "

"I know, Papa But it helps me to hurry if a big meal is waiting at home," Andrew replied with a crooked grin.

Kirsten tried to hide her smile. Andrew was so refreshingly honest at times. If only Peter were less reticent and silent. One never knew what the solemn dark teenager was thinking.

All the way to church Sunday morning Kirsten wondered if Wilshire Patten would remember his promise to drop by the farm on his way to Washington, for two weeks had gone by since her fall from the horse. Then she dismissed the thought. She was grateful that her ankle had healed. There wasn't even a trace of a limp.

After Papa had parked the wagon on the west side of the church and had tied the team to one of the sturdy walnut limbs of the West Woods, the family hurried toward the small house of worship. Allie Mumma, her eyes sparkling with merriment, waved to Kirsten from the doorway. The women used the south entrance and seated themselves in the pews to the left while the men came in the east door and sat at the right.

The presiding elder and visiting preachers

sat on the long pew along the north wall facing the altar table and congregation, Papa among them for the first time. He looked so spiritual, so pious, with his neatly trimmed dark beard and black coat with its upright collar. The plain wooden altar was adorned only with a large German Bible and an earthenware pitcher and glass for water used by the presiding elder. The most devout members of the church usually sat near the front.

Kirsten's white net cap or "prayer covering" sat pertly on her rich coiled brown hair, her ringlets tucked snugly away from her face. Her dark blue-black dress, like that of the other sisters in the congregation was cut simply, with a high neckline and full skirt. As she started toward the front rows with Lelo and Heidi behind her, she turned her head for a moment to see if Peter and Andrew had found their pews. Across the aisle sat David Poffenberger, his blond hair neatly combed and his heavy beard trimmed, his gaze on the presiding elder and a gentle smile on his lips.

Then Kirsten's gaze froze. There, behind David, tall and handsomer than she remembered, sat Dr. Wilshire Patten, dressed casually in brown riding breeches and deep tan shirt open at the throat. On his feet were polished brown boots. He seemed to focus his eyes on the neatly lettered German Scripture verse in Gothic script hanging on the front wall of the church: *Der Herr Ist Mein Hirte.*

She felt her cheeks blaze with color and she sat down quickly, motioning to her sisters to scoot silently beside her. So Wilshire Patten had come after all. And had the — audacity, was it? — to attend church services he had disdained as "boring." Her heart pounded frantically under the dark blue poplin bosom. Her lips, softly pink and full, were parted, and she breathed more heavily than usual.

She tried to concentrate on the hymns, the verses Elder Mumma read from the huge German Bible, but all she could muster was a feigned look of interest. Dear God, she prayed, what's wrong with me? Why do I feel so — so disembodied? If only the service was over and she could flee before the young doctor stopped her.

Elder Mumma's message of God's love droned on and on. Usually she reveled in the glory of knowing God loved her and that he had accepted her as his child when she had prayed, in faith believing. But now — !

Kirsten clenched and unclenched her hands, hiding them under the hymnal on her lap. Her gaze strayed across the middle aisle surreptitiously. A fly buzzed through the open windows and lit upon Daniel Miller's bald head. She tore her eyes away, catching a brief glimpse of Wil Patten's rapt face. Was the look a cynical one?

When the service finally ended and the parting hymn fell like a soothing benediction on the congregation, Kirsten bowed her head swiftly. "Forgive me, Father," she prayed, "for being so inattentive. But why did you permit this stranger to upset me?"

She almost ran from the building toward the wagon in an effort to avoid meeting him, pulling Heidi with her. It was best he didn't see her.

"What's your — hurry, Kirsten?" Heidi panted. "We didn't stop to shake hands or greet anyone. Not even Allie!"

"Don't you remember?" Kirsten hissed in Heidi's ear. "Papa said we were to hurry home."

"But not *that fast!* As if you were trying to avoid someone — "

"Kirsten?" Andrew's young voice called out behind her. "Guess who's here. Dr. Patten — and he wants to see you."

Slowly Kirsten turned and waited with pounding heart as Wil Patten came toward her. She noticed his eyes were very blue, and he seemed even taller close up than she remembered. He held out his hand toward her, but she could only stare at him. He reached for her fingers, gently raising them to his lips.

What's he doing? she thought wildly, jerking her hand away. Then she took a deep breath.

"Doctor — Patten," she murmured in a low voice, "I — I'm so surprised. . . ."

"But I said I'd come, Kirsten," he said with a throats' chuckle. "Surely you haven't forgotten?"

Her father came toward them, replacing the big broad-brimmed black hat on his head.

"Kirsten," he said in his strong, authoritative voice, "did you know this stranger who attended our services today?"

Kirsten nodded, her throat choked up. "Papa — this — this is Dr. Wilshire Patten — the medical student who was there when I was thrown from Polly. Remember? I told you about him. He — "

"How do you do, sir?" Wil reached for Papa's hand and clasped it strongly. "I told your daughter that, when I returned from Hagerstown on my way back to the capital, I would stop by to check on my patient, to see if her ankle has healed." His blue eyes twinkled, as if it were some queer joke. "Perhaps she didn't believe me!"

Papa's gaze was guarded as he shook the young man's hand. "Oh, yes, of course. You were most kind. She has recovered completely, thanks to your capable help." His words sounded like a curt dismissal.

Kirsten squirmed, her legs trembling and her lips dry. Finally she opened her mouth. "I — I wasn't sure what you meant," she stammered politely. Suddenly she wanted to make up for her rude behavior. "Perhaps — perhaps you'd like to eat with us? It's the least we can do to show our appreciation. . . ." *Surely he'll refuse,* she thought, *but I had to say it. He would be in a hurry —*

"Why, yes, I'd be delighted," he said. "I'll get my horse and follow you home."

Papa raised questioning eyes to Kirsten's but she turned away quickly. She never knew how she made it back to the farm with Papa's cold silence taunting her. Her mind spun in circles, thinking of the plain lunch she had prepared that morning. How could she offer Wil Patten anything so simple and countrified?

While Papa took Wil's hat and laid it on the small table near the front door, Peter politely invited their guest to the plainly furnished parlor with its brown horsehair sofa and sturdy maple rockers. Kirsten flew about the kitchen, hurriedly putting the finishing touches on dinner. She nervously ordered Heidi and Lelo to set the table with the best blue willoware china and stemmed amber water glasses.

The main course consisted of hearty beef stew swimming with generous chunks of carrots and turnips, a large bowl of boiled squash mashed with sweet butter from the cave and dotted with clots of cream, thick slabs of fresh-baked wheat bread, and late garden tomatoes sliced on a blue platter. The dinner was topped with apple pie from early Jonathans that simmered with sugary juices and flavored with cinnamon.

Wil was lavish in his praise of the meal. If he thought it mediocre, he hid it well.

"This food's fit for the gods," he said, finally pushing back his chair. "It makes one forget the war that's being fought beyond the Potomac."

"Perhaps we here will be able to forget about it," Papa said stiffly. "We Dunkers believe war is wrong, you see. The Scriptures plainly tell us to love our enemies. How did you enjoy our services this morning?" he added, raising one eyebrow piously.

Wil lowered his gaze, then looked straight at Kirsten. "It was — I'm not familiar with your order of worship. Furthermore, it seems hard to believe that God would see fit to redeem this wicked world. I, for one, cannot understand such love for mankind. Maybe it's all right for folk like you who live simply, but — "

"It's only as man sees his need for God's love that salvation is offered," Papa said fervently. "As our church motto proclaims — "

"I do not understand German," Wil interrupted dryly. "Those words in that quaint artistic Gothic script. . . ."

"'The Lord is my Shepherd,'" Kirsten said. "We believe it — claim its promises."

She arose and refilled the coffee cups, her hands shaking. *I should have known,* she told herself as she sat down again at the table. *To him, our ways are quaint, simplistic.*

"But when one sees the real world as it's lived around us — the horror of war. . . ." Wil's words trailed away. "How *can* a just God condone it?" he added with a fierce shake of his head, the pucker between his brows standing out sharply.

The silence at the table grew ominous, and Kirsten toyed with the hem of the red checkered cloth. He would probably be called up to fight and he knew the horror of it.

"You could refuse to serve in the army,

couldn't you?" she said in a thin voice. "As a doctor — "

"As a doctor I'd be needed on the battlefield. I could refuse but I won't. Not if my country needs me."

Suddenly he pushed himself away from the table and got up. Kirsten was on her feet instantly, and moved toward him.

"You must leave?" she said, her voice low. Did she want him to go away, knowing she would never see him again?

"I must move on, if I'm to reach Washington in time for tomorrow's classes," he said, looking deeply into Kirsten's gray eyes. "It's a long, nearly seventy-mile ride." He took her hands in his and held them for a moment. "Thank you, Kirsten, for a delicious meal and a delightful time. I see your ankle is fine." Then he turned to Kirsten's father, and raised his hand in a faint salute. "And thank you for your kind hospitality, sir. If I can ever be of further help — "

"That won't be necessary," Papa said coldly.

Then Wil strode to the table and picked up his hat and was gone.

Kirsten watched him go. Would she ever see him again? For some unknown reason her gray eyes blurred with tears, and then she was aware of Papa's gaze upon her.

"Kirsten," he said, his look strong and forbidding, "does this young man mean anything to you? You invited him — "

"Oh, Papa — no!" she denied vehemently. "He — no, of course not. I was only being — kind."

But she could feel the betraying red color seep into her cheeks.

3

Fall had stolen in quietly and the wooded valley lay shrouded in autumn haze. Creeping vines on the peeling whitewashed bricks of the house were aflame with frost-rich scarlet. Hayfields to the southwest lay like a shimmering tawny sea flecked with emerald and purple.

Kirsten and Lieselotte had spent busy weeks scrubbing the huge old house to scour away the summer's grime. In spite of Lelo's grumbling the two girls had completed the job on schedule. The cave in the hill below the house looked like a jewel case with its bins of carrots, squash, potatoes, onions, and pumpkins the girls had harvested. Later smoked hams, sausages, and crocks of lard would be added to their winter stores.

In the bedroom Kirsten changed into a fresh dark blue frock and brushed her rich brown hair into thick coils. Then she set her little black bonnet on her head and tied the narrow ebony ribbons under her soft white chin and turned to Lelo who was watching her.

"You'll make out all right when I'm gone." Kirsten picked up her sewing basket. "Remember to scald the milk before you whip up the potatoes for dinner."

Lelo scowled as she straightened the embroidered scarf on the chest of drawers.

"You taught me all that when you played the Dutchess last summer," she pouted. "Please give me credit for remembering something."

"I'm sorry, Lelo, but I'm so used to taking charge — "

"Run along to Allie's. Although I don't envy you the job of tying all those mounds of comforts and stitching miles of bed clothes. But I guess it's up to you to take Mama's place in the sewing society."

"You're right. Taking full responsibility for my family — "

"You've done right well, Kirsten. Be careful so Polly won't throw you this time. That handsome young doctor will hardly be around the same place twice to rescue you!"

Kirsten blushed, then grabbed her gray wrap and hurried down the stairs and out of the house. She was relieved that Wil Patten hadn't written, yet a bit disappointed, for it was hard to sort out her feelings toward him. He excited and moved her as no man had ever done before; yet she knew deep in her heart that, as a Christian and a member of the Dunker Church, she had no right feeling anything but friendship toward the polished young medical student whose life differed so vastly from hers. Of course, she told herself his concern for her was only as a patient.

She rode down the narrow winding trail that led toward the church, then turned northeast from the Hagerstown turnpike between the split rail fences, and a quarter of a mile down the Smoketown Road to the substantial Mumma farm. Just to the left lay the naked East Woods, already bereft of brilliant fall colors.

The farmhouse, tall and imposing, was built of oven-dried brick as were most of the farm homes of the German Baptist Brethren. It was Allie's father who had donated the land for the church, and it wasn't unusual to call it the "Mumma Church."

Since the charitable work had been organized, the women met regularly to tie comforts and sew sheets and other bed linens for the needy. Among the cabins in the Blue

Ridge Mountains a real need for goods of this kind existed, and the Society was capably working to help meet this need. In the absence of her mother, Kirsten felt it her duty to help. Especially today when the Society met at the Mumma farm and she could visit her friend Allie at the same time.

The two girls greeted each other affectionately, laughing as they joined Lizzie Grove beside the tall, square windows facing the lane.

"I wonder how those mountain folk tuck these sheets over their straw mattresses," Allie bubbled. Sometimes Allie came up with the queerest notions. Like now, for instance.

Lizzie, Allie's older sister, snorted delicately. "Pshaw! What does it matter? It's our Christian duty to help these people where their needs are, not to speculate how they're used!"

"I know, Lizzie. But sometimes I wish I was a little mouse and could travel along with the goods to see what happens," Allie protested. "Don't you, Kirsten? Don't you ever?"

Kirsten laughed. "No, I don't think I ever have. The Scriptures tell us we're not to let the right hand know what the left hand is doing. Besides, I'd rather have the good feeling of helping someone."

"You're right, Kirsten. We'll probably never know. But when I think of how that fancy young medical student made it a point to find out how *you* were doing, after you hurt your ankle — "

"That — was different," Kirsten cut in quickly. "It was a — a medical problem. Doctors are supposed to follow up on their patients, aren't they?" She bent her head down low over the sheet that shrouded her lap, and covered her hands to hide the pink that suffused her cheeks.

"Well, all I know is that he was the hand-somest man I ever saw," Allie said, biting her thread. "And if he were a member of the church, I'm sure David would have reason to worry."

"David? He hasn't even asked if he can visit," Kirsten snapped. "So of course, he has no cause to worry."

"Oh, you disgust me," Lizzie snorted. "You remind me of an auctioneer: 'How much am I bid for David Poffenberger?' Why not leave that in God's hands?"

"But God gives us common sense too, Lizzie," Allie said, pausing to thread her needle. "Sometimes we must give him a boost!"

The three fell silent for a few minutes. In

47

the background, Mrs. Mumma was busy with dinner preparations for her guests and Lizzie got up to help her mother.

Kirsten wondered how Lelo and Heidi were coping with the noon meal at home. There was always plenty to eat, but Lelo was dreamy and flighty and Kirsten sometimes worried that the shapely blond would never quite learn.

Allie laid down her white cotton square and touched Kirsten's shoulder. "Let's run out for some fresh air," she said. With a nod, Kirsten went for her wrap and black bonnet, and the two girls set out. The Mumma farm sat astride a low hill that sloped into gray valleys and fields now rattling with dry cornstalks.

Allie flung her arms wide. "How I love this place," she said fervently. "I hope I never have to leave it!"

"But what if you got married?"

"Well, in that case I'd ask my husband to come live with me!" And the two girls laughed hilariously. Then Allie sobered. "Sometimes it scares me a little. What if the Confederates cross the Potomac into Maryland? What will happen to us? General Lee has boasted he'll invade the North — even into Maryland."

"I know General Scott is getting too old

to serve as commander of the Union Army," Kirsten shrugged, "and McClellan and Sherman have their differences. All this squabbling makes it easier for the Rebels."

"My father says that if McClellan were in complete charge, the Federal army could get the job done in a hurry. He did order General Stone to provoke the Confederates into action, didn't he?"

Kirsten sighed, recalling Wil Patten's words about Little Mac's cautiousness. "But remember what happened at Ball's Bluff? Colonel Baker was killed and his men panicked. The command is too divided, and that's what worries me."

The two strolled down the path in silence. The trees of the East Wood stood bare and naked, and fields beyond brown and empty. In the draw a shallow creek rilled its way toward the Antietam farther south. The air grew chill, and Kirsten drew her wrap closer.

"We'd better go back to the house," Allie said suddenly. "Our sheets won't get hemmed if we don't get back to them," she added with a lilting laugh.

"And the mountain folk will never know you worried about them!" Kirsten chuckled.

They shrugged off their momentary fears

and hurried back into the large pleasant farmhouse.

As the day drew to a close, Kirsten said her good-byes and rode home to fix supper.

Papa was full of questions during the meal. "How does it look to you, daughter? Will the Society have a wagonload of goods ready for distribution before Christmas?"

Kirsten laughed a little. "Not so fast, Papa. Our fingers fly as fast as possible, but we aren't machines. It's possible the Manor Church sisters will help. Have you contacted their elders? If they agree — "

"The Manor Church elders?" he cut in. "Why, that's a splendid idea. I'll visit them first thing in the morning. Peter, can you handle the stacking by yourself?"

Peter looked up from his cornmeal mush. "You've taught me well, Papa. I can do anything on this farm you can," he muttered.

"Good. Andrew knows his way around the stock by now, don't you, son?"

"Sure, Papa," Andrew mumbled, his mouth full of fried apples. "Did you know that the Daniel Millers are building a new storage bin for their corn?"

"How'd you know? Sure, they had a surplus of corn — "

"I sort of snooped. It doesn't take much to figure that out when they haul extra brick onto their yard. When I check my traps — "

"Andrew — what about school?" Kirsten cut in sharply.

"We were dismissed early." He looked at her sheepishly. "Sorry, Kirsten. I forgot to give you a message. I met David — you know George Poffenberger's David. He said to tell you he plans to stop by tomorrow afternoon."

Kirsten drew in her breath quickly. So Allie was right. David was planning to visit her. The news wasn't exactly breathtaking, although she knew she should be dancing at the prospect of seeing the most eligible young man in church.

"I'll make sure the washing's out of the way," she said simply.

"Are you — " Papa began with interest, "are you thinking of leaving us, Kirsten? We've come to depend upon you so."

"I have no plans for leaving for a long time, Papa," she said tersely. "For as long as you need me, I'll be here."

Kirsten argued with herself all morning the next day as she rubbed Papa's blue chambray shirts on the washboard. What was wrong with her? Just because David was stopping by was no sign he had marriage on his mind. Still, she was nineteen, the age many young women already rocked cradles and nursed infants. It was time she was interested in romance. But it was out of the question.

When David rode up on his brown sorrel, the clean, scrubbed wash was flapping in the brisk afternoon breeze and her rich brown hair freshly combed and coiled in her neck.

David had never looked finer. His sandy beard was neatly trimmed, not bushy as some Baptist Brethren wore theirs. His cheeks were firm and ruddy, and hard muscles rippled along his strong arms. He was a clean, shining young man, brown as the September fields. To marry a man like David Poffenberger was probably the romantic aim of every young girl in the church.

She served coffee and apple schnitzel in the parlor as they visited. There was talk of war but David wasn't worried, he said.

"As long as the Confederates stay in Virginia we have no cause for alarm. Yet I must admit that I'd feel safer if we weren't so near the Potomac."

They talked of the church, of the community, of the crops too. She knew David worked hard on his father's grain farm.

"What I really came to talk about, Kirsten . . ." he said suddenly, "I feel the Lord would give us his blessing if we — you and I —

were to marry. We're so well suited to each other. I'm not asking for a definite answer now, but please think about it."

Kirsten drew in her breath sharply. How like David to be so practical and direct! She smiled a little and set down her coffee cup on the sturdy oak table beside the sofa where she sat.

"I'm flattered, David, that you should ask me. But I'm in no hurry. Papa depends on me in so many ways since Mama is gone, and I can't think — of leaving my family," she faltered. "I must confess I haven't given much thought to love."

"I understand, Kirsten. But promise me you will consider this proposal seriously?"

Kirsten hesitated. *At least I could tell him I'll think about it,* she thought. He'd be a fine husband and she would never have a care in the world as his wife. She opened her mouth to tell him so, then closed it again. Then she gulped.

"Thank you, David. I'm — flattered, please believe me. But as long as Papa and my family need me, I must put all thoughts of love and romance away. I couldn't ask you to wait until I was — ready." Something in the back of her mind nagged at her. *This isn't the real reason. You're doing a reasonable job in training the flighty Lelo to take over the house-*

hold, and Papa could count on Peter to look after the big outdoor jobs. You're not as in-dispensable as you think, Kirsten Weber.

Then why am I hesitating? she thought. Was she still thinking of the tall young doctor when she knew the idea was so utterly ridiculous?

4

Mid-November winds blew in with cold, hard sunsets and sycamores snapping with frost in the South Woods. For days the drowsy dripping of rain had shrouded the secluded farm in great folds of gray. Calves fretted and cried in their pens as Andrew, donned in a black slicker too long for his short body, fed the livestock while Peter forked down hay from the loft.

Papa, bent over boxes and barrels, nailed them securely before loading them into the large, rough-board wagon. Kirsten stood by the tall, narrow south window and watched. Lulled by the dreary drumming rain and purring of flames in the huge fireplace, she sighed a little as she turned away and started for the kitchen. She had put the reluctant Lelo to work sewing quilt scraps while Heidi pared potatoes for dinner.

Papa decided to take a load of supplies

for the needy down to Harper's Ferry before winter weather set in, praying for a
boat to haul them up the Shenandoah
River to the railroad that ran with gleaming silver rails toward Manassas Gap and
the blue mountains of the west. The
Manor Church elders had brought boxes
of supplies so that, together with the quilts
and sheets the Mumma Society had made,
the first load was now ready to leave. Just
how he would maneuver the heavy wagon
along the surrounding terrain, Kirsten did-
n't know, for Harper's Ferry was dominated by mountainous bluffs that fringed
the town. But Papa said he knew of a way.
And knowing how stubborn Papa could
be, Kirsten was sure she couldn't talk him
out of it.

With a loud stomping on the porch, Papa
burst into the house, shaking the drops from
his broad-brimmed black hat as he shrugged
out of his wet jacket.

"I'm all packed up and ready," he said as
he held his hands to the open fire. "If I go
now I'll be back in three or four days. Think
you and Peter can manage by yourselves
while I'm gone, Kirsten?"

She took his damp coat and draped it over
a chair. "Yes, Papa. I'm sure we'll be fine."

"You know how I depend upon you,

daughter. I'm proud of the way you helped with the sewing."

"We know it's for a good cause." She paused a little. "You won't be in any danger, Papa?"

"Not a bit. The arsenal at Harper's Ferry is safe in Union hands again. And the trip is less than 18 miles. I'll be back before you know it."

"I hope so, Papa. With this damp weather you could get chilled. Danger of pneumonia haunts us each winter, you know."

Papa laughed. "I'm a strong German, Kirsten. And the prayers of God's people will go with me. I've been elected by the church to be in charge of the charitable work and dare not shirk my duty." His face took on its pious mien.

Although he was lean and spare, Papa's body was strong and hale. There was no need to worry, if he said so.

The rain had finally stopped and only a few ragged clouds scudded across the clear sky. At midmorning the wagon lumbered down the lane and disappeared from sight. Kirsten turned to the family still gathered in the house after saying good-bye.

"Now Papa is gone . . . we must all pull together until he gets back," she said, a shade of authority in her voice. "Peter, you oil the harness while Andrew and Heidi fill the woodbin. It's getting low. Lelo, you'll help me give Papa's bedroom a good airing while he's away."

"In this damp weather?" Lelo pouted. "I'd hoped we could pop some corn and sit around and read. I haven't even seen Papa's latest church journals!"

"Just because Papa isn't home doesn't mean we can lie down on the job," Kirsten said sharply. If Lelo had her way, she'd fritter away her hours dreaming or reading. Then softening, she added, "We'll eat an early evening meal, then play some games. Maybe we can pop some corn too."

Peter gave her a long, searching glance and started for the door. "You and Papa always have the answers for everything!" Then he slammed out of the house and went toward the barns.

As Kirsten and Lelo cleaned and mopped Papa's room with its plain walnut bed and highly polished dresser, Kirsten thought about Peter. He had always been quiet and rather sullen, but she had never thought much about his taciturn behavior. *I wish I knew what was bothering him,* she thought.

Her chance to talk to him came sooner than she expected. She had slipped into her heavy jacket and taken the slop pail with potato peelings and dishwater out to the hogs when he crossed the yard on his way to the grain bin.

"Finished with the chores?" she called out.

He came toward her slowly and stopped. "All done. I could do it all in my sleep — it's so easy. Everything's too easy here on the farm," he said in a low, tight voice.

"And — and you don't like the easy life?" she parried. "I know many people would."

Taking off his wide-brimmed hat, he twirled it absently in his short, stubby hands. "I don't mean *easy* that way, Kirsten. But why is it decreed that Baptist Brethren must be farmers?"

"And you don't like farming? I thought perhaps some day you'd take over — "

"I would like to be — to be a — a teacher. Or a — a lawyer, maybe, Kirsten."

"A lawyer!" Kirsten cried, steadying herself against the split rail fence. "You know we don't hold with — with all that book-learning. Not when farming's in our blood. Besides, the church frowns on too much education."

"Well, farming isn't in mine," he snapped. "All I know is that I want to do something else with my life. But Papa would never accept that." His words were bitter.

For a long minute Kirsten was silent. Poor Peter — and poor Papa. Peter tried so hard to be loyal; he bit back his true feelings because he was afraid to disappoint his father. And yet —

Slowly she slid an arm through his, and looked up into his deep gray eyes. "Peter, if this is what you want . . . somehow, some way we'll have to make Papa understand."

"But now that he's an elder he'll be busier with the church than ever. He'll never be able to spare me." He shrugged off her arm.

Silently Kirsten picked up the empty pail and headed for the house. Maybe after an evening of popcorn and checkers Peter's spirits would lift. And anyway, she couldn't deal with the problem alone. Papa would have to be told sooner or later.

Kirsten lit the lamp and set it on the dining table after the family finished its meal of fried ham and baked beans. The room flickered and danced with shadows. Andrew pulled the checker game from the sideboard drawer and set it on the table just as a rap sounded on the front door.

"I wonder who it is," Kirsten said, pouring melted butter over the corn she had popped. It wasn't unusual for neighbors to drop by in the evening.

When Peter opened the door, David

Poffenberger stepped inside. His ruddy bearded face was red with cold, and drawing off his jacket he hung it on the hook near the door.

"Come join in some family fun," Kirsten said. "The evenings without Papa can be lonesome."

"I'm sure they are. That's why I came — to offer my help in case of need," he said, his green-gray eyes crinkling into ready laughter. "I saw him leave for Harper's Ferry today."

"Yes. He takes his church responsibilities very seriously," Kirsten told him, pulling out a chair at the table for him.

"He should be back before the weather turns nasty," Peter said. "Not much we can't handle."

"But with all the unrest in the country," David cut in sharply, "let's face it. The war may be coming closer than we think. I suppose you've heard that General McClellan is now General-in-Chief of the United States Army?"

"With a real celebration, including a torchlight parade in the capital," Peter added suavely. "Bands and everything. It must've been quite an event."

"And another big air balloon sailed over the Potomac," Andrew said, his hand fingering his black chesspiece. "How I'd like to fly in one of those. It would be a new way of exploring the countryside."

"You!" Heidi spat out. "Andrew Weber, you — you snooper! There isn't an inch of the South Woods you haven't already explored."

"Or the West Woods either," he reminded her with a lopsided grin. "If you set traps you got to know where they are."

"As long as the North knows what the South is up to," sniffed Lelo, "maybe General McClellan can get this war over in a hurry."

The evening passed with gay banter and laughter and munching bowls of light, buttery popcorn.

Suddenly David glanced at the Seth Thomas clock that ticked on the mantel above the fireplace, and jumped to his feet.

"Look where time has flown," he said, bowing to Kirsten as he started for the door. "But it's been a pleasant evening. Thanks for the popcorn. And remember to call on me when you need help."

After he had left, Lelo drew a deep sigh. "If I was reading between the lines, I'd say David Poffenberger was here for more than popcorn." She looked slyly at Kirsten. "Or didn't you notice? But I hope you remember your promise to Papa."

A slow wave of color seeped into Kirsten's cheeks. She'd been so sure David understood that she couldn't leave her family.

"Don't worry," she said jadedly. "I'm not ready to — to marry for a long time. To David or to — to anyone else." Then her lips twisted bitterly. As though there could be anyone else.

5

In less than a week Papa was back, just before winter set in and the weeks lengthened into December. The air was heavy, the sky gray and cold like a winter's pond. The trunks of the sycamores in the South Woods stood out white and naked. To the west, stark arches of the hills flanked the Potomac.

Kirsten, scattering corn for her flock of squawking ducks, shivered in her short brown jacket. The noisy cackle of hens and roosters broke into a cacophony of sound all around. From the woods came the ring of axes, for work on the farm never came to a standstill even in cold weather. The men always had wood piles to replenish, harness for the heavy work horses to oil and mend, or repairs to make on the sheds and barns. And the never-ending work of checking split rail fences. Even rock fences had to be mended occasionally. Indoors, too, Kirsten and Lieselotte whisked about from dawn to dusk with cooking, cleaning, washing, ironing, mending. But Papa insisted the girls attend sewing bees wherever the Society met — if items were being made for the charity project.

Today they would drive out to the Daniel Miller farm that lay a half mile north of the church along the Hagerstown Pike. The turnpike, built only a few years ago, clattered sturdily with farm wagons and the sharp clink of rider hoofbeats as daily traffic moved between Hagerstown and Sharpsburg and the towns scattered farther south.

Kirsten, with the reins in her hands, clucked to the team as the carriage rumbled down the pike. At Papa's insistence, Lelo had joined the sewing society, although the young girl had demurred.

"As though I don't have enough chance to prick my fingers on the piles of mending at home," she grumbled.

"But think of the things we're making for the poor," Kirsten tried to encourage her. "God has blessed us with so much, and those underprivileged hill folk have nothing."

"Well, I wish we'd hurry and reach the

Millers' soon," she said, her teeth chattering. "I'm almost frozen solid. I could've stayed home and cooked dinner for Papa and Peter."

Kirsten turned to face her sharply. "I suppose so. But you probably wouldn't have done anything else. Not as long as there's a book you haven't read! Besides, I fixed a big kettle of beef stew and left it simmering over the fireplace."

Andrew and Heidi were back in school after a long recess when children were needed to help bring in the fall crops.

As the carriage clattered up the lane toward the large, two-story many-windowed Miller farmhouse, Kirsten looked around for one of the men to come stable the team.

Just then one of the hired hands hurried from the barns, swinging his gloved fists jauntily as he walked.

"Hello!" he called out cheerily. "Here. Give me the reins, and I'll tie up the team before I help you ladies from the carriage."

As he bowed and doffed his soft gray cap, a riot of auburn curls tumbled over the broad forehead. His eyes were a deep brown, clean and gentle as a collie's. He wore mustard-colored trousers and a warm plaid wool jacket.

First he helped Kirsten to the ground, and

as she thanked him and turned toward the porch, she noticed that he seemed in no hurry to let go of Lelo's hands while lifting her from the vehicle. Her sister seemed mesmerized by the polite young man.

For a few minutes Kirsten stood and watched. The two seemed to be taking their time in the transition, then Kirsten caught the sparkle in Lelo's blue eyes as she clung to the young man's hands.

"Lelo!" Kirsten called sharply, waiting on the steps. "You'd better come indoors where it's warm. You said you were cold, remember?"

Lelo jerked her head quickly. "Coming, Kirsten!" And with a gay wave of her mittened hand, she scrambled up the steps.

Kirsten's forehead puckered into a frown. Lelo acts as though she's just met — Her face flamed. Almost the way I felt when I met Wilshire Patten. . . .

With a quick tug, she pulled her sister through the door into the large, warm kitchen, as though trying to push away the thought of the handsome young doctor.

Mrs. Miller rushed toward them. "Girls! How good that you both came!" she gushed. "With your nimble fingers, we should finish many a seam today." She took their wraps and black bonnets as she shepherded them into the large room beyond where bolts of cloth, snip of scissors, and chattering voices dominated the scene.

"Mrs. Miller," Kirsten said before joining the other women, "who is your new hand? I don't think I've ever seen him before. Or in church either."

"Oh, no doubt you haven't. His name is Martin Druse. The Druses have moved on a farm near Keedysville. We've needed extra help this fall with the corn and all and he's very capable. The Druses attend the Lutheran Church in Sharpsburg."

"I see." Out of one corner of her eyes Kirsten watched her sister who had turned away casually, but she was sure Lelo had absorbed every word.

Soon the hum of voices and clicking of needles filled the morning. To Kirsten's dismay, Allie Mumma wasn't there.

"She's helping Lizzie with some Christmas sewing," Mrs. Mumma informed her. "Before you know it, the big day will be here."

Christmas. Kirsten bit her underlip thoughtfully. She had secretly knitted socks and scarves for the menfolk, and made a pretty apron for Lelo. *I must finish the new blue wool outfit for Heidi's doll,* she reminded herself firmly.

Lelo's pouty pucker between her eyebrows had vanished and the girl chattered as her hands flew with a needle.

On the way home Lelo eyed Kirsten slyly. "Well, what did you think?"

"What did I think about what?"

"Martin — the young hand. Didn't he seem — nice? And so delightful. I mean — he's not from the church, but have you ever met anyone more polite?"

Kirsten laughed out loud. "So that's what this is all about. It's too soon to tell — from those few brief moments he lifted you from the carriage! But — yes, he did seem nice. And now that you've met him, you'd better forget about him."

"But why? Kirsten, what's the matter with you?"

"You're too young to be thinking of courtship and marriage, Lelo."

Lelo's mittened hands clenched on her lap. "But you — you're thinking of it. If not that handsome young doctor, then — David Poffenberger."

"And I'm not planning to marry either of them," Kirsten snapped. "As you've pointed out — my family needs me!"

Lelo fell silent, and the carriage creaked down the dim trail around the bend toward the secluded farm in the hills. Already long shadows stretched away from the lowering sun.

Christmas dawned gloomy and gray. The family ate a hearty breakfast of hot porridge and fried sausages before opening their gifts and driving to Christmas Day services at the church.

Kirsten tried to push away the dismal thoughts that had crowded her mind. Ever since the sewing bee at the Millers', she had felt a vague sense of uneasiness. It was nothing to which she could point her finger. Was it because her sister was entertaining romantic thoughts while she should be denied them? As Papa had reminded her often, he depended on her.

The Christmas service was simple and brief. The story from Luke 2 had reminded the small cluster of worshipers that Jesus Christ had come as a baby in a manger to become their Redeemer and Lord. It was as plain as that.

After the roast beef dinner and dishes, the family scattered to their own devices. Papa lay down for a nap while Peter settled before the fire with the newspaper. Andrew and Heidi bent their heads over a game of checkers. Where Lelo had disappeared to, Kirsten had no idea.

She felt a need for a brisk walk in the cold

outdoors, and slipping into her warmest garments, she chose a heavy dark green knitted scarf for her head instead of her usual black bonnet, and set out toward the South Woods.

Dry leaves made crunching sounds underfoot as she walked between the sycamores and maples. Snatches of blue iris in the cloudy skies cleared and widened, and with it the wind rose. Kirsten pulled her wrap around her shoulders as she walked slowly among the bare, gaunt trees, her head bent.

Hearing a sharp snap behind her, she whirled around. Immediately she saw the familiar black stallion, hooves thudding on the crackling leaves, and then she looked up at its rider. Wil Patten sat tall and straight in the saddle, wearing a heavy leather jacket, his brown head bared, the familiar slight pucker between his dark eyebrows. He smiled, and the neatly trimmed mustache twitched slightly.

"If I want to see you, I must hunt you down, my dear," he said, pulling the horse to a stop beside her. "As I was coming around the bend I saw you heading for the woods. Tell me, is it for a secret rendezvous?"

"A — what? Oh, you mean — am I meeting anyone?" she lifted her chin firmly, "Most decidedly not!"

"Oh, but you're wrong. I'm here, and this gives us a chance to talk undisturbed."

I won't let myself get all worked up this time, she decided. *My heart will not race and pound —*

"What's there to talk about?" she said, her voice cool. "If it's my ankle you've come to check — "

"I see very well that it's fine," he said. "It shows what a good doctor I am!"

Her lips tugged into a faint smile. "I'm sure you are. But why else?"

He slid from his horse in one quick motion and came toward her. "Kirsten, I had to come. You see, I — " He spread out his hands helplessly, "I just can't get you out of my mind. I think of you day and night. There's no forgetting you."

Kirsten's heart began to hammer in spite of her determination, and she clenched her fists, shivering as she tried to calm herself.

"You're cold," he said softly. "Here, let me — " He reached for her and drew her against him gently. "Kirsten. . . . Oh, Kirsten, I must say it," he whispered against her ear. "Kirsten, I love you."

With a sudden jerk she pulled away. "No!" The word caught in her throat and almost strangled her. "Please, Wil — no! You can't — you can't love me. We — we're so different. Don't you see?"

He placed his arms on her shoulders and faced her. "There's no bridge we can't cross if we love each other, is there?"

"You — what does my Christ mean to you?" she said huskily. "The church — you said yourself you couldn't accept our teaching."

"Please believe me, Kirsten. I've thought about it," he said with a deep sigh. "But as a scientist I cannot believe that there's redemption in the simple act of Christ's death on a cross. It doesn't make sense — it's too incredible!"

"I'm sorry." She pushed his hands away. "But that's the very essence of Christianity! Please don't say any more, for I'll never change."

He stood looking at her and his eyes, more deeply blue than she remembered, were full of pain. "Kirsten — Kirsten, my darling. Don't — please don't push me away. I wish it were different, but all I know is that I love you!"

Heartache and weariness swept over her, and she dropped her head on her gloved hands and began to cry. He reached out his fingers, touched her cheeks, and pushed back a stray lock of hair.

Then his arms went around her and

73

pulled her close. She dropped her head against his shoulder, hearing the beat of his heart. She felt his hard muscles beneath his coat, his cheek against her hair, the strong arms that held her as if he would never let her go. She could not pull away, to run from him. When he bent his head toward her, his lips sought and demanded, and he held her so tightly she could not free herself. For one delicious heartbeat, she let the moment envelop her. Every rational thought was blocked out, every guilty feeling. Then with a strangled sob she tore herself free, her eyes blazing.

"Please — don't ever do that again!"

"But — " he looked bewildered. "Kirsten? . . . Your kiss. . . ."

She shook her head so violently that the heavy scarf fell from her shoulders. "No! No, I — I can't — I just can't. It — it was only a — a foolish whim when I got carried away. Please."

He turned away slowly and started for Beecher who stood with head lowered to the ground, nuzzling the dry carpet of leaves.

"I'll write, Kirsten," Wil called out hoarsely as he swung onto the saddle. "I'll keep in touch." Then he wheeled his horse around and rode away.

Kirsten watched him go, and a pain like

that of a knife twisted in her heart. She rubbed her lips, as though wiping away his passionate kisses. Write? she thought bitterly. She knew she could never answer his letters.

6

The new year of 1862 arrived in the teeth of a hard, biting wind that drove dark clouds swiftly across its face, rattled windowpanes, and moaned faintly about the house. The months of January and February boasted of slate skies and snow that fell light and soft as the cat feet of winter, settling on houses and sheds, and penciling bare branches with thin white lines, and piling into deep, mauve-tinted drifts.

News from the war front trickled into the community and was discussed around barrel stoves in Sharpsburg stores, or wherever its citizens met. The troops were mostly in winter quarters during January, although there were light skirmishes at Bethel, Virginia, as Union soldiers seized the town and the Confederates fell back. In Washington there was a growing concern as General McClellan appeared reluctant to commit his troops to concentrated action. A group of harried senators approached President Lincoln with suggestions that Little Mac be replaced but the President rejected the proposal. He strongly recommended that Union forces advance in order to provide support for east Tennessee.

Secretary of War Simon Cameron resigned and was replaced with Edwin Stanton, an antislavery friend of McClellan's. . . . In the capitol at Richmond, a scant hundred miles from Washington, the Confederate House delegates entered into a debate concerning black enlistments in the Southern army. Some observers worried that the Southerners were growing tired and were not "sufficiently alive to the necessity of exertion."

In February, President Lincoln's 12-year-old son Willie died of typhoid fever. This personal sorrow compounded by the news of fatalities at Fort Donelson in Tennessee laid an even greater weight on the thin, stalwart shoulders of the tall, beleaguered leader. . . . Jefferson Davis was elected president of the Confederacy after having served as provisionary president. On February 22, when he was inaugurated, he said, "We are in arms to renew such sacrifices as our fathers made, to the holy cause of constitutional liberty."

In March, John Minor Bott, an avowed neutral, was seized with 30 others, and tried for treason against the Confederacy. President Lincoln tried to devise ways to abolish slavery and Robert E. Lee was given responsibility of overseeing Rebel forces. . . .

Kirsten grew weary of the reports that only seemed to create graver problems for the divided country. She worried about Peter, who had grown more sullen and quiet as the weeks dragged by.

One day he caught her just as she went out to the woodpile to fill the basket of chips.

"Have you spoken to Papa yet?" he asked, his dark eyes somber and shadowed.

"Peter, you're barely eighteen," she reminded him, picking up the basket and balancing it on her knees. "You may change your mind a dozen times about leaving the farm. . . ."

"No, Kirsten. I'm fed up with farm work. If Papa would only let me try something else."

As she started for the house with her basket filled, she called out over her shoulder. "Give me a bit more time. I'll see what I can do."

His scowl frightened her, but she tried to push it from her mind. As if she didn't have enough troubles of her own, running the household, attending church sewing bees, and looking after the family, without taking on Peter's problems too. And trying to ignore Wil Patten's letters.

He had written several times. Mostly Peter or Andrew went after the post, and twice she had been to Sharpsburg to pick up the mail herself. He had told her that his courses at the medical school were quite difficult but that his scores were good.

"Whenever I take a particularly hard test, I remember your lovely face, and it gives me courage," he wrote in his last letter.

True to the promise she had made to herself, she had not answered his letters. He must put me out of his mind, she vowed. But it wasn't at all easy to forget him. There was something tender, so lovable about him, although she had seen the stubborn glint in his steely blue eyes.

Now as she carried the wood into the lean-to behind the kitchen and dumped it into the bin, her thoughts again returned to Peter. What should she say? How could she convince Papa when she didn't know how to solve her own problems? For a moment she entertained the thought of asking Wil Patten for advice about her brother, then dismissed the idea quickly. What did Dr. Patten know about loyalty to the church and its long-established mores?

Dear Lord, she prayed. *Please show me what to do. How can I best help Peter?*

Lieselotte used every feminine wile she could think of to visit the Daniel Miller farm but Kirsten was adamant.

"You're not some brazen hussy to throw yourself at Martin Druse!" she flared. "If it's God's will that you two meet, then so be it. But I'll have no part in all this."

Heidi was like a ray of sunshine. Always cheerful and willing to do as asked, the child had learned quickly how to iron the stiffly starched clothes almost as well as Kirsten herself.

"When can I start wearing prayer caps, Kirsten?" she asked one mild afternoon when the two sisters hung white, billowing sheets on the clotheslines.

"When you become a member of the church," Kirsten told her. "After the weather warms, there'll be a baptism in the Antietam. But you're still too young."

"Sometimes it's hard to wait to grow up," Heidi said, shaking out a hemstitched pillowslip before pinning it to the line. "If I hurry up and learn to do your work, you can marry David."

"Marry — David!" Kirsten almost choked

on the clothespin clamped between her teeth. "But who says — "

"He's so much fun. When he comes over, he always asks to play checkers with me."

Kirsten hung up Peter's blue shirt. "And he lets you win, too," she chuckled.

"That's more than Andrew does. Besides, Andrew's busy with his traps or chores after school and never has time to play with me anymore. So I might as well grow up."

Kirsten laughed. Heidi's refreshing candor was exactly what she needed today.

" — hope he'll come over tonight?" Heidi's chatter half-escaped Kirsten.

"What did you say? Oh, you mean, if David comes over tonight," Kirsten said.

"David Poffenberger likes you, Kirsten. But so does Doctor Patten, doesn't he?"

Kirsten made a small choking sound. "I — I can't think of marrying for a long time. Papa and the rest of you need me. Besides — " her voice trailed off. "Doctor Patten is — is only interested in my — my ankle," she added lamely, wiping away the memory of his kisses on Christmas Day.

And that, she told herself decisively, *is the way it's got to be.*

"Well, then, that leaves David," Heidi pronounced as she danced away.

That night David came by as usual, and

81

the checkerboard appeared as if by magic. Papa had gone to the Samuel Mumma farm for a meeting of church elders. Kirsten observed David's lean, ruddy face in the yellow lamplight and watched the strong, thick work-worn hands that moved the chess pieces along. Kirsten knew why he had come, but there was no way she could leave her family, and she smiled a little at Heidi's devotion and her hurry to grow up so Kirsten could marry. But even if she could, she wasn't sure she would marry David.

"I guess you've heard that the president and General McClellan have made plans for the Army of the Potomac," he said after his usual game with Heidi ended in her scooping most of the blacks into her pile. "It's important that some Federal troops be stationed at our capital."

Peter looked up from the paper he was reading. "And won't that draw strength from the standing army?"

"Some soldiers must protect Washington while the rest attack the Confederate capital at Richmond, I suppose."

Peter gazed steadily into the fire, his face thoughtful. "That will take many Union soldiers," he said in a slow voice. "A great many."

"But that doesn't concern us," David said

briskly. "Our job is to farm our land and raise good crops. As pacifists we needn't worry about the fighting." He pushed back his chair and got to his feet. "I suppose it's time to go," he said, stretching his arms. Then he looked directly at Kirsten. "Unless you want me to stay."

Kirsten drew her breath sharply. She hated to encourage him by urging him to remain but she must be tactful.

"That's up to you, David. Why not visit with Peter while I see that Heidi and Andrew have their warm milk? They insist they can't sleep without it."

She hurried into the kitchen. I hope I wasn't rude, she thought, pouring milk from a white earthenware pitcher into a small kettle. She didn't want to think about the love light she had seen in David's pale, gray-green eyes.

When she returned to the dining room, David was gone. Lelo had followed Heidi and Andrew upstairs and only Peter sat at the fire, his newspaper folded on his lap. Kirsten thought he looked deeply troubled. But of course, Peter had seemed unhappy for a long time.

"Kirsten," he said suddenly, "I've been thinking. I must do something with my life. With the need for soldiers in the Union army, what if I signed up to help Little Mac in the Army of the Potomac?"

Kirsten felt the color drain from her face. *Peter — a soldier! How preposterous! Why, he was just a boy —*

"I'm eighteen, and I know what I'm doing," he said stoutly, as though guessing at her response.

Finally she found her voice. "Peter — what are you thinking of? The church — you know we're pacifists. We believe fighting is wrong. Promise me you won't do anything until we've talked to Papa?"

A sullen look crossed his face. "I know his answer before I even say one word," he said bitterly. For a few moments he stared at the crackling fire, then he nodded. "I know you're right, but you've no idea how I hate to plow and sow and harvest. If only Papa would understand."

Kirsten steadied herself against a chair, her legs suddenly weak. She too knew what Papa's answer would be.

Swallowing hard, she said, "We — we'll have to hope and pray for the best. Good night, Peter." She walked toward the stairs and began to mount them heavily.

7

April stole in quietly. The orchards flaunted pink and white nosegays shafted with fragrance while hills and valleys spread out soft green skirts over the spring landscape. White clouds moved leisurely across the sky like scrubbed sheep grazing on a blue meadow.

In his last letter, Wil told Kirsten of completing his medical studies. She was in the kitchen, rolling out a crust for sweet potato pie when Andrew brought in the letter.

Wiping her floury hands, she sat down to read it. "I must admit I've done well," he wrote. "So well, in fact, that I've been offered a teaching fellowship, training other medical students proper surgical procedures. However, at present I've declined. The Union army needs surgeons desperately, and I've decided to join McClellan along the Potomac. Kirsten, I've waited so long for a letter from you. Although I do understand your reluctance to write, I know how you feel about my faith — or lack of it. Please write to me! When I remember your kisses — soft and sweet. . . ."

Kirsten crumpled the letter into her hot fist, tears brimming from her gray eyes. She wiped them with a corner of her apron, trying as well to wipe out the memory of Christmas day. Peter sauntered into the room, dark brow furrowed as usual, and threw himself into a chair across the table.

"Bad news, Kirsten?"

She sighed as she chewed on her lower lip. "Oh, Peter, everything's all mixed up. I had another letter from Wil — Dr. Patten. Of course, I haven't answered any of them. He's completed his medical studies and will join McClellan's army. He could've avoided this by accepting a teaching fellowship."

"Would it have made any difference to you if he had?"

"Oh, I don't know. No, I guess not. Either way, I — he — we could never . . ." her words trailed away.

"I suppose Papa would object if you decided to marry him," Peter said a shade contemptuously. "At least, Patten can make his own choices."

"But Peter," she cried, "don't you see? Wil

doesn't share our faith. And besides, I could never leave the family. Papa depends upon me for everything."

"Not even for David?"

"Not even for David."

He stared pensively at her for a long minute, then nodded curtly. "Well, you've made up your mind, but I'm not supposed to know mine!" His tone was harsh.

"Please don't say that, Peter."

"I guess you've enough problems of your own without trying to see my point of view," he said, abruptly getting to his feet. "I might as well go out and finish planting corn, like a proper German Baptist Dunker!" With that he grabbed his broad-brimmed hat and stalked from the room.

I must talk to Papa, Kirsten told herself firmly. Peter is growing more morose and bitter every day. She'd have to pray that he would change his attitude about farming.

It wasn't until the next morning when she was on her way to the hen house for fresh eggs that she had a chance to waylay her father as he came from the shed, carrying a bucket of feed.

"Papa — " she called out rather hesitantly, "Papa, I must talk to you."

He paused, and looked at her sharply. "Is it about David Poffenberger? I notice he's been here often lately. If you're thinking of getting married — "

"It's not about David — it's Peter."

"Peter? What's that boy been telling you? That I must keep after him and keep after him to finish planting corn?"

"Papa, Peter feels he — Peter is unhappy about being made to farm. He would rather do something else."

"Unhappy about farming?" Papa's face clouded. "But that's what all Baptist Brethren do. It's our lifestyle. Peter knows that!"

"Yes, he knows that, but it doesn't mean he has to like it," Kirsten said. "He's — he has even hinted at joining the — the army. I've told him — "

"Join the army!" Albert Weber's face was livid. "We're pacifists! He knows better than that. Well, I'll forbid any such nonsense. He's on the farm and that's where he stays!" With that, he stomped away.

Kirsten watched him go, her heart aching for her brother. Well, she'd tried. She also knew Papa would be fiercely angry if he knew she was receiving letters from young Dr. Patten. Oh, why were things so hard? Spring should be a happy time of hopes and dreams, of being full of the joy of working and living. Instead, the grim specter of war loomed on the horizon, she was tied to her family, Peter was unhappy — and the man she cared about most was not for her. She must do something to keep from thinking. It was high time to plant a garden.

Andrew and Heidi wielded hoes all morning, and their laughter and chatter helped take Kirsten's mind from her overwhelming problems. But by lunchtime they were tired of the monotonous chore.

"We've planted enough potatoes to feed an army," Andrew grouched when the last tuber had been pushed into the ground and covered with soil.

"And I've sowed so many peas that all I'll do this summer is snap pods," Heidi muttered in response.

"Well, you're both probably right," Kirsten said wearily, picking up the hoe and empty sacks. "But when the wind howls next winter, you'll be mighty happy with our food supply in the cave."

Just then Lelo came running out to meet them, her full gray skirts blowing in the wind. "Kirsten, Papa says we're to go to Sharpsburg for more materials to sew for the charities. If you're finished — "

"But I thought you didn't like sewing," Kirsten cut in, handing the hoes to Andrew. "Here, put the garden tools away before you check the calves. And you, Heidi — take the clothes from the lines and fold them." She turned to Lelo. "Are we to go now?"

"Right after lunch. Papa said Peter could drive us in the wagon. No, I still don't like sewing but going to town will break into my boring day. Do you realize I baked five loaves of bread and six pies this morning? Anything for a change of scene."

Hurrying indoors, Kirsten changed into a clean dark blue dress and rearranged the coils of her brown hair. She was glad Papa had asked Peter to go. Perhaps her father had more sympathy for Peter than she had thought.

An hour later the three young people set out for town. As the wagon rumbled and creaked down the road, Kirsten eyed her brother surreptitiously.

"I'm glad Papa asked you to take us," she said. "It's a good break from your work in the fields."

"I guess so," he said passively. "But of course, I'm to buy another sack or two of corn, so I'll have more work!"

The ride was pleasant in spite of his morose response. Meadow larks warbled from split rail fences and clusters of wild violets peeped from the green grass that grew along the roadside. Now and then a startled rabbit scurried across the road, white tail bobbing like a ball of cotton.

"When will Papa take another load of goods to Harper's Ferry, do you think?" Lelo asked, her dancing blue eyes focusing on the outskirts of town.

"He plans on a load in another month or so, as soon as the summer farm work is done," Peter said, clucking to the team as it slowed on the edge of town. "That's why he wants the bed linens ready."

Minutes later he reined in the team before Elias Smith's store. "While you buy what you need, I'll pick up the corn at the mill," he said as Kirsten and Lelo climbed from the wagon. "Be back in an hour." With that, he clucked to the team and drove off.

A mixture of odors rushed out to meet the two girls as they stepped inside. Kegs of molasses, smoked herring and codfish, sacks of dried crabapples, and the usual barrels of crackers and pickles cluttered the store.

Kirsten hurried toward the shelves at the rear that held bolts of cloth, Lelo at her heels. She fingered the dark blue calicoes and red-checkered ginghams carefully. They'd also need several bolts of muslin for sheets.

"Must you buy so much muslin, Kirsten?" Lelo muttered in her ear. "If there's anything I hate worse than hemming sheets. . . . There's no room for imagination!"

"Sheets?" A warm voice spoke behind them. "Oh, how delightful. I think it's commendable that you Baptist Brethren ladies sew to help the needy."

Kirsten turned. The middle-aged woman who spoke looked neat and trim in a simple green-sprigged lawn with a dainty white ruffled collar. Her honey-colored hair was parted in the middle and half-covered with a pink slat bonnet. Her merry blue eyes twinkled from shaggy dark brows.

"Oh?" Kirsten drew her breath sharply. "Why — why, yes, we feel it's the least we can do to help the less fortunate. I'm Kirsten Weber and this is my sister Lelo — Lieselotte. We — "

"Yes, we keep busy with sewing," Lelo bubbled with false enthusiasm.

"And I'm Carrie Druse. We live on a farm near Keedysville. It's good to meet you." She thrust out a work-worn hand. "You people are so — so dedicated and I think it's wonderful how you serve the Lord. Martin says — he's our son who's been helping Daniel Millers — he says there aren't any better people on the face of the earth than the Dunkers."

At Lelo's sharp, indrawn breath, Kirsten

paused. So this was Martin Druse' mother. Then turning quickly to the woman she nodded. "Yes, the Lord is good," she said lamely, not quite knowing how to respond. "If the war weren't so near our doorstep — "

"It seems there's a real need for soldiers. Martin threatens every day to enlist. General Beauregard is counting on every available soldier possible to win this war."

General Beauregard! But he's a Confederate general, Kirsten thought. Most Marylanders were Union sympathizers. Then Martin Druse was — Kirsten turned her face away, unwilling to look at Lelo. She fumbled with the list in her hands, hardly knowing what to say.

"I guess — I guess there's lots of trouble — in this world," she gulped finally.

The woman moved toward the counter with her purchases. "Yes. But as you say, the Lord is good to his children. Well, I'd better finish my shopping." With that, she began to pick up her items.

Kirsten turned to look at Lelo, and her heart twisted at the stricken white face. Lelo flew toward her and buried her head against Kirsten's shoulders.

"Oh, Kirsten — it's hard to believe — Martin a — a Rebel! And he was so — so nice. He — "

"There are good people in the Confederacy, Lelo," Kirsten said gently. "Don't take this so hard. Christians too. Mrs. Druse seems like a woman of deep faith."

Kirsten tried to sound reassuring but she knew this had hit her sister hard.

Soon Peter's wagon rumbled up to the hitching post. He helped carry their purchases out and with a clatter and rumble of the team and wagon they were off.

Lelo's usual merry chatter was absent, and Kirsten couldn't blame her sister. The trio was quiet on the short ride home. Only when he turned around the bend did Peter speak.

"At the mill I heard about the Battle of Shiloh," he said quietly. "The losses were staggering. The Union Army lost over thirteen thousand men."

"Thirteen thousand! Which — which side won?" Lelo asked, her voice high-pitched and anxious.

"There was no conclusive victory for either side."

8

May drifted into June in a blaze of sunshine and a maze of growing crops. The Federal push toward Richmond continued under General McClellan's command. As usual, Little Mac was overly cautious so that President Lincoln pressed him to "either attack Richmond or give up the job and come to the defense of Washington."

News continued to seep in from the capital. The President had outlined his controversial Emancipation Proclamation, outlawing slavery in all states that continued to rebel against the Federal government.

All Kirsten's letters from Wilshire Patten had ceased, and she told herself it was for the best. Yet no matter how she tried, she couldn't erase the handsome young doctor from her mind.

Peter was more quiet than ever although he worked in the fields faithfully.

"If I didn't suspect he was harboring a secret plan," Kirsten told herself one day, "I could almost feel he had decided to give in to Papa."

Between hoeing the large, thriving garden, drying bushels of peas on the tool-shed roof, and looking after the countless household chores, Kirsten worked hard on the pile of sewing that Papa insisted must be finished before his wagon trip to the nearest railroad.

"We must get the supplies to their destination before the armies tear up the tracks," he said as the girls worked feverishly on the growing stacks of sheets and pieced comforts. The whole community seemed gripped in a state of restlessness. Kirsten sensed it every time she went to the store. It was as though they lived in an uneasy dread of something no one could put into words.

Lelo, in spite of her shattered dreams of Martin, moved about in her usual world of fantasy. When she thought Kirsten wasn't watching, she opened her honey-blond braids and let them spill down her shapely shoulders.

I should scold her for it, Kirsten thought, *for entertaining worldly feelings.* Still, it might not hurt Lelo to indulge in a few innocuous dreams. She certainly hadn't inherited Kirsten's practical streak. In spite of her fantasies Lelo didn't shirk her duties.

"I'll do what's necessary if it kills me," she burst out one day after Kirsten had praised her for a particularly neat seam she was sewing, "knowing the Society will chalk up good marks on my behalf."

"I do appreciate your attitude," Kirsten remarked dryly. "Even though your motives aren't the purest."

They both laughed over that. Heidi drifted in and out of the house, between helping her older sisters with the housework and rambling with Andrew on his walks over the countryside on Saturdays.

"Daniel Miller has the best forty-acre corn patch in the County," Andrew remarked candidly one afternoon when the twosome returned from their walk. He doffed his straw hat and fanned his sweaty face.

"You know who planted it, don't you?" Lelo said, her blue eyes shining.

"If you mean that new hand, Martin Druse," Andrew smirked. "Well, maybe he did. But he quit last week to sign up with General Hood, I hear."

Kirsten stole a quick glance at Lelo and saw her sister's face whiten. So he had finally made good his threats to join the Rebel army.

Most of the Brethren, although espousing pacifism, leaned toward the Union; yet it was no secret that some Marylanders were fiercely Southern sympathizers.

Peter broke down when he heard the news of the battle of Gaines' Mill, the third of the series in the Seven Days' Campaign. He and Kirsten were feeding calves in the corrals one warm evening in early July.

"If there was only something I could do to help." He shook his head as he told Kirsten the grim news. "Anything at all."

"Peter — " she spoke slowly, evenly, "I've told you, as a member of the church, you know fighting is wrong. We can pray and we can sympathize, but beyond that — "

"There's the ambulance corps. I could go as an orderly, helping with the wounded — "

"I still say it's not our way, Peter."

She turned away, not willing to see the pain in his dark eyes. Pouring the last bucketful of dried corn into the trough she hurried back to the house. I can't face him now, she thought desperately. All I can do is pray. Maybe he's right, but I can't let him do it, Of course, he would mope and sulk and glower, but when he saw that she needed him after Papa left with his load of supplies he would see that his duty lay with his family.

To take her mind off the war and Papa's impending trip a few days later, Kirsten hastily planned a Fourth of July picnic. This 86th celebration of Independence Day was being observed with greater enthusiasm in the community than usual.

"We'll pack a lunch and go out to the West Woods and celebrate our country's freedom," she told Andrew and Heidi who seemed more excited about the prospect than she had anticipated. She was packing cold ham and boiled eggs into a straw basket, with generous slices of whole wheat bread.

"Can we wave flags," Andrew said, "and pop a few crackers?"

Lelo curled her lips at the thought. "Better not shoot anything, Andrew. Some folks might think the Rebels have attacked."

"Awl, Lelo," Heidi scoffed, "I don't think anybody'd invade our peaceful countryside. What would they get out of it?"

"You mean — Martin," Andrew muttered, and Lelo shot a vengeful look at her brother.

Papa came into the kitchen just as Kirsten tucked a clean tea towel over the food. He eyed the basket shrewdly. "What is all this about, Kirsten? Do you think it's wise?"

"All we hear is war talk," she cut in. "We need time for fun."

"Yes, of course." He nodded absently and laid his big hat on the table. "As long as you finish the sewing I must take with the shipment."

"Most everything is done, Papa. You're to stop by the Mumma farm and pick up their barrels and boxes. Altogether with what the Manor Church has provided, it should make a good-sized wagonload."

"As soon as we finish the grain harvest," Papa said, picking up his hat and heading for the door.

Kirsten dreaded to think of Papa's leaving. She knew the responsibility for the family and farm would rest on her shoulders and she drew a heavy sigh. *I don't know how I can do it,* she thought. But she knew she would. There was no other way. *Papa would be gone only a few weeks — if that long. He had promised to be back soon.*

But as the days passed, word came that Harper's Ferry was being considered a Confederate target again.

"Then I must take the goods to Washington," Papa said with a determined jut to his jaw. "The wheat is in the bin. I must get these supplies to those who need them as soon as possible."

Kirsten felt a chill sweep over her at his words. It wasn't a feeling she could describe. But she couldn't help believing that the forthcoming weeks would somehow change her life — all their lives.

9

"I can't believe it!" Papa strode into the house, frantically waving a letter in front of Kirsten.

She looked up from the dark gray sock she was darning. "What is it, Papa?"

"Andrew brought a letter. It's from Harris Shoe Factory in Hagerstown. It seems they've heard of our charitable work and have offered us a barrel of shoes — if we go after them."

He sat down, drew off his big black hat, and ran squat fingers through his graying hair.

"But why? Is there a catch?"

"None whatsoever. It seems these shoes are somewhat — mismatched or the leather was not tanned properly or something. The owner doesn't want to sell them to respectable customers, so he says that if the mountain folk won't mind wearing them, we can have them. Isn't God good?"

"Yes, that's wonderful," Kirsten said, snipping the gray yarn with her shears. "But what's this about going after them?"

"Jonathan Harris says they'll be over at the house, and that's where we're to pick them up." He looked expectantly at Kirsten. "I want you to go with me."

"Me?" Her gray eyes widened. "But why, Papa? Why can't you get them yourself? What could I do to help?"

"According to Jonathan Harris, it's his wife's idea, and she wants to meet — the Baptist Brethren who're involved in this charitable work. There's to be a tea, so I need you, Kirsten, a woman — to go with me. As a proper gesture, we must pay a visit to this austere benefactress."

"But — what do I know about meeting rich, proper ladies, Papa?"

"All I know is that I'll trust your womanly instincts about the right way to behave before worldly ladies. Kirsten — you must go with me!"

She laid down her darning needle and skein of yarn and moistened her lips with her tongue.

"You know, I have no more experience in meeting people of the world than you, Papa — and except for Wilshire Patten, I don't know anyone above our social level."

"I'll feel better, knowing a female is with me. Now, change into your best blue dress and get out your dress bonnet while I harness the team. We'll take the carriage."

He picked up his hat and stalked out of the house. Kirsten breathed a deep sigh. It wasn't as simple as Papa seemed to think. How could she cope with meeting a socialite like Mrs. Jonathan Harris? Slowly she went upstairs to pull on her best dress and comb her hair into a neat bun. Lelo followed her into the bedroom.

"What's going on, Kirsten?" she asked. "I overheard Papa telling you to put on your finest things while he gets out the carriage."

"It seems some wealthy shoe manufacturer in Hagerstown is offering a barrel of shoes for our charities, and we're to pick them up — and stay for tea in their fine home. Oh, Lelo, I'm so — flustered!"

Lelo's blue eyes danced. "Kirsten, what I wouldn't give to visit one of those fancy homes! If only Papa had asked me to go with him."

"No, Lelo," Kirsten said archly, "you're too flighty. God knows what ideas you might pick up there." She paused, then went on, "I didn't finish mending Peter's socks and he will need a clean pair tomorrow. So you'll have to finish — "

"How can you be so mean, Kirsten?" Lelo flared. Then she touched Kirsten's shoulders. "I'm sorry. But you know how I hate to wield a needle. I'll tell you what. If you'll positively tell me everything when you come home, I'll finish Peter's socks. I'll even start supper."

Kirsten smiled wryly. "Thank you, Lelo. I'll try to remember everything." With that she drew on her black bonnet and hurried out to the waiting carriage.

The ride in the light conveyance behind the spirited horses took slightly less than an hour. The afternoon was warm and to Kirsten's dismay, her dress, which had been fresh and crisply starched and ironed when they left, now clung damp and wilted to her body.

As they rode down Hagerstown's paved streets lined with fine, two-storied brick mansions, Kirsten's heart hammered with fear and trepidation. If only she wouldn't make a fool of herself in front of the fabulous Mrs. Harris.

The carriage drew up before a high red brick wall with a wrought-iron gate. Papa peered at the number on the gatepost.

"This is it," he said, and clucked the team into the wide, shaded drive. As she alighted, a strange feeling swept over Kirsten. It was as though she had stepped into another world. The well-kept garden ran down to the river. There were two lawns divided by a path of crazy paving. One lawn was dotted with shrubs and masses of Michaelmas daisies like lovely mauve stars, and a riot of gold-tipped chrysanthemums.

The path led to the house that stood three stories tall of the same red brick as the wall. The door was iron-studded, and the high, graceful windows latticed.

Her father pulled the rope and an old bell clanged hollowly through the house. After a brief wait, a young maid opened it and dropped a flustered curtsy.

"Come in," she said in a breathless voice. "I'll get Mrs. Harris," and hurried away.

Kirsten glanced around. The house had enormous rooms, high ceilings, ornate woodwork, hand-carved scrolls over wide double doors that opened from the expansive hallway. Fine, smooth floors made of sturdy oak seemed to have worn well over the years. The winding, carpeted staircase was lined with tapestries and a few good oil paintings.

Suddenly a tall, slender woman came from the rear of the house. Her medium brown hair streaked with gray was pulled straight back from her big strong face, and knotted into a bun behind her head. She wore a gray tweed skirt and a severe olive green waist, the same color of her eyes. As she came forward she stretched out her hands.

"You must be Mr. Weber of Sharpsburg," she said warmly as Papa drew off his big black hat awkwardly. "And you?" she asked, turning to Kirsten.

"I'm — Kirsten, the oldest of the five Weber children."

"Oh, yes, of course. Come into the library where we can talk."

Kirsten followed their hostess into a dark, elaborate, high-ceiled room with a large brick fireplace at one end. The windows were open to a rapidly warming breeze where sheer creamy scrim curtains dallied gently. An exquisite piece of tapestry hung on the east wall, and along book-lined walls stood several dusty-rose softly upholstered chairs. Mrs. Harris motioned them to sit down.

Kirsten sank into a chair and primly removed her black bonnet, her curls feathering around her face. Papa sat down across from her.

"Now," Mrs. Harris said briskly, "I know you've come for the barrel of shoes. When I learned of your charitable ministries to the people in the Blue Ridge hills we decided to help. It's a most worthy cause."

"Yes, Mrs. Harris," Papa said politely. "We feel God wants us to help the less fortunate. It was most kind of you to offer the footwear."

Mrs. Harris laughed heartily and somehow Kirsten felt her laughter sounded familiar. Where had she heard it before?

"Please remember — the shoes are perfectly wearable. But some are flawed due to the tanning process of the leather and we couldn't market them through the stores. So I told my husband that I'd heard about the charitable work you Dunkers are doing, and in a small way we could help."

"That was very generous of you," Kirsten said. "Tell me — who told you about us — about our work among the needy?"

"My son Wil. He's ridden through Washington County to the capital time after time. He's very impressed."

At the mention of the son's name Kirsten felt color drain from her cheeks, and she drew her breath sharply.

"Your — your son?" Kirsten faltered. Of course, there could be a thousand Wils.

"Yes. Wilshire studied medicine in Georgetown University. He's serving in General McClellan's army under Dr. Dunn at present. Do you know him?"

Kirsten moistened her dry lips again. No wonder the woman seemed vaguely familiar. There was her laugh — and something about her that was so like Wil.

"He — he treated me when I was thrown from my horse last summer. He — he's an excellent doctor."

"And a brilliant surgeon!" Mrs. Harris added with a throaty laugh. "Of course, being his mother I could be prejudiced. But his professors offer great hopes for a promising medical career in his future."

Papa splayed his palms nervously on his knees. "He was most kind. But — the name? Harris?"

"Oh. Wil's father died when he was a small lad. I married Jonathan Harris a year or so later. We've given Wil every opportunity to join the family business but he always wanted to help people. Wil is an only child."

No wonder he seemed so polished, so self-assured, Kirsten thought. It was easy to see that Wilshire Patten had had wealth and prestige to back him in his pursuits.

The flustered maid brought in a tea tray, bowed, and left without a word. Mrs. Harris arose from her chair and poured tea into fragile china cups.

"Tina is new here. With the war, some

soldiers' wives are forced to support their families, but Tina's trying! Sugar or cream?"

Kirsten shook her head. She still wasn't over the shock of being in Wilshire Patten's home where lifestyles were so vastly different from those of the simple German Baptist Brethren. Yet Mrs. Harris was gracious and kind, and in no way did she make Kirsten and her father feel they were "different."

The time spent over tea and cakes was filled with small talk, and with little mention of the war. At the end of an hour, Papa got stiffly to his feet.

"It's time to move on, Mrs. Harris. It will soon be dark. Again, let me thank you and your husband for your kindness. Surely the Lord will reward you for it."

Mrs. Harris took his proffered hand. "But we didn't do it for the rewards," she said in a gentle voice. "We just wanted to help." Turning to Kirsten, she placed a warm hand on the dark blue shoulder. "And to you, my dear, God's very best. It's a pleasure to meet one of Wil's satisfied patients!"

As they moved toward the door. Kirsten donned her bonnet and turned around for one final glance at the lavish surroundings, trying to place Wilshire Patten here as a lad, running up the wide stairs, and being waited on by family servants.

Then without another look she told Mrs. Harris goodbye and followed Papa to the carriage where two men servants were loading the barrel of shoes in the rear.

As they rumbled away from the elaborately furnished streets, Papa turned to her.

"Well, daughter, what did you make of it?"

"Make of what, Papa? The — the affluency, the wealth? Or their thoughtful gesture in providing the shoe barrel?"

Papa clucked to the team and they started on a gallop on the outskirts of town. "Their way of life is so very different from ours, Kirsten. Yet Dr. Patten's mother's heart seemed tuned to God's voice in doing good. I'm grateful for that. Only God knows what's in their hearts."

The sun was lowering in the west in a vivid display of color as the carriage clattered down the pike. Kirsten closed her eyes and leaned back her head. She felt the stiff black bonnet against the hard leather cushions. Could she ever give up wearing black bonnets and long-sleeved dark dresses and be waited on in a mansion as Wil had? She shook her head slowly. *I know where I belong,* she told herself firmly. *With my people. . . .*

came at all? Papa had asked. If he left immediately he would encounter no real danger, he was told.

Papa rushed home in a flurry of plans. "I must leave right away," he said that hot morning when the August heat hung motionless in the air. Not a breath of wind stirred, and the ominous quietness seemed to presage a coming storm. "I'll come back as soon as I can," he repeated when Kirsten eyed him anxiously.

She nodded, her hair sagging listlessly from its pins. "I'll pack some food for you to eat along the way," she said, now that the day of his leaving was actually here. "Where will you sleep at night?"

"People are kind. Or I can always spread out a blanket in some haystack," he added. "Once I arrive in Washington I'll check into some inn until my business is finished."

"Yes, Papa."

Kirsten had never been to Washington, and she had no idea what the inns were like. Surely they were clean.

She packed several chunks of smoked ham and loaves of bread into the straw basket, and added a dozen ripe apples from the orchard. She worked quietly, her mind on a dozen things at once. The wheat was harvested and taken to the mill, and large bags

1

Fears were growing stronger that the Confederate Army would march toward Maryland and on into Pennsylvania. Papa went to Sharpsburg and asked questions. Yes, there were rumors, he was told, but no real evidence. Ever since the Baltimore riots early in the war, there had been more signs of pro-Confederate sympathy in the state. Lee had written to Confederate President Jefferson Davis, saying that the presence of troops in Maryland might afford the state "an opportunity of throwing off the oppression to which she is now subject." Yet no concrete plans for invasion had crystallized. General Lee surmised that General Halleck's and General McClellan's armies were far apart, and his hope was to beat Pope before Pope joined Little Mac.

Would he have time to go to Washington and back before the Rebels came — if they ground into flour for bread; the haying was finished and stacked neatly in cone-shapes near the barns; the fields were plowed for winter fallow. Papa promised to be back in plenty of time to pick corn. Peter would have little to do but mend fences and the everyday chores. They would get along.

When the wagon was packed and ready to leave, the family gathered around Papa for tearful good-byes.

"I pray God will keep you all safely," he said, hugging each one in turn. "Don't forget I'll be back in less than three weeks, if all goes well."

Kirsten fought back the tears. She knew these would be the longest three weeks of her life.

After bidding the family good-bye, he turned to Kirsten. "Remember, I'm counting on you to take care of things until I come back. I know I can depend on you. Don't forget to trust God, and promise me you'll stay here, no matter what."

"I — promise," Kirsten said, her voice thick with tears. "You'll be all right?"

"I'll be fine, knowing I'm doing the job the church has entrusted to me." Turning to Peter, he patted the thin shoulders, then climbed onto his wagon. "And you, Peter, I know I can trust you to stand by Kirsten."

With that, he clucked at the team and drove slowly down the lane. Lelo and Heidi hurried back into the house and Andrew sauntered toward the barns. Kirsten waited silently until the wagon had disappeared around the bend. The feeling of desolation swept over her again, and she leaned unsteadily against Peter's rigid body.

"Oh, Peter — I'm so glad you're here!" she cried. "Somehow I feel so alone."

"Oh, you're strong, Kirsten. You'll weather anything," he said as though to remind her. He gripped her shoulders tightly and gave her a quick squeeze.

"Maybe." The word was unsure. "I suppose there's nothing to worry about, is there?"

"Not a thing!" Peter grinned at her, swung around almost jauntily, and followed Andrew toward the barns.

Squaring her shoulders, Kirsten went into the house. The breakfast dishes still sat on the table, for Papa had been in a hurry to leave. She heard Lelo and Heidi upstairs making beds, and she began to scrape the plates and stacked cups and carried them into the kitchen.

The first week of Papa's absence dragged by without incidence, and they were well into the second. Kirsten tried to keep busy with the house and garden, and helped Peter and Andrew with the farm chores. Peter seemed almost carefree, and she couldn't understand it. Was it because he no longer felt Papa's thumb suppressing his need to get away?

When President Lincoln issued orders to draft 300,000 men, Peter grew agitated, and it disturbed Kirsten.

That the order didn't go into effect relieved her somewhat, but the same look of eager anticipation shone in his dark eyes.

"Have you checked the fences?" she asked one morning right after breakfast while they still sat around the table. "We can't afford to lose any stock."

"Oh, me and Peter have been over every square inch," Andrew burst out. "I could'a shot a dozen rabbits if I'd had my gun with me."

"Good thing you didn't. Who wants rabbit stew when we have plenty of food in the cave?" Peter growled amicably. He backed away from the table and picked up his hat. "Come on, Andrew. Let's go to the South Woods and chop up some of those dead trees. Kirsten will need lots of wood for cooking."

"The woodpile is still the size of South Mountain," Heidi scoffed. "I ought to know.

I fill the woodbox every night."

Peter grunted and looked sharply at Kirsten. "Anything you need me for? Any jobs that need doing? Clotheslines tightened? Utensils mended?"

Kirsten eyed him covertly. "Thank you — no, Peter. Just make sure the farm chores are taken care of. Have you boys hoed the corn this week? I know how important it is to keep ahead of the weeds."

"And to keep ahead of the Millers' fabulous cornfield. Come on, Andrew."

As the two brothers slammed out of the house, Kirsten frowned. She couldn't understand what had gotten into Peter. No grumbling. It was almost as though he had decided he liked farming after all.

Lelo stood in the kitchen doorway and placed her hands on her plump hips. "Peter sounds — strange," she said suddenly. "I'm not sure I like it."

"So you've noticed it too. Well, I've prayed that the Lord would make him content. Maybe he's decided to earn the trust Papa placed on him before he left."

"I hope that's all it is," Lelo said. "I was getting tired of his sulking and pouting."

"We all were." Kirsten pushed away from the table and began stacking plates. "Well, I guess we'd better get on with the day's work.

Today we'll pick some early apples and make up a batch of applesauce."

Lelo frowned. "Apples! Kirsten, don't you know what peeling those tart things does to my hands?" She spread out her pretty dimpled palms. "They were beginning to look right nice again, after that last batch of cucumbers we placed in brine."

Kirsten laughed. "Look at mine." She turned over her rough, red hands. "I declare, Lelo. What else can you expect from a farm woman?"

"Well, I guess David Poffenberger doesn't mind if your hands look rough. But what of Dr. Patten?" Lelo began to carry dishes toward the kitchen.

"Doctor — But why should Wil Patten care about my hands? You know I'll most likely never see him again." The words came out a trifle wistfully and she chided herself.

"Well, if all you told me about his family in Hagerstown is true — and the fancy mansion they live in — Kirsten, are you sure all this didn't affect you?" Lelo demanded.

Kirsten didn't answer. She had to put the young physician out of her mind. At the dogs' sudden bark, she walked toward the window and drew back the white ruffled curtains. She saw David tie his horse at the hitching post and come up the path to the front door.

What does he want? she thought. *Of course, as a neighbor he needed no excuse to come over. Perhaps he came to see Peter about some farm work.*

At his sharp rap, Kirsten opened the screen door. "Come in, David. If you want to see Peter, he and Andrew are hoeing corn."

"I stopped to tell you to call on me for any help while your father is gone." He doffed his broad-brimmed hat and his tawny hair drooped over his forehead.

"Sit down, please," Kirsten said politely, shoving a chair toward him. He remained standing, and she stood with her hands clutching the back of the chair.

"No, thank you. But I hope you won't forget to call me, Kirsten." He lowered his gray-green eyes, then turned to her with his infectious grin. "I can't tell you how much your father's taking this load of supplies to Washington means to the church. Elder Mumma remarked to me just yesterday, no one but a dedicated man of God would leave his family in these dangerous times to perform his mission."

She nodded. "Yes, Papa is very dedicated. Do — do you think there's any real danger? I mean — there have been so many rumors — "

"We all feel uneasy with the war looming closer, and the Confederates are growing bold. Just a few days ago General Stonewall Jackson held off Pope's army. In fact, Pope has lost his field, his reputation, plus 15,000 men. These aren't rumors, Kirsten. These are facts." His smile vanished with his words.

Kirsten clutched the back of the chair, her knuckles white. "Papa has been gone nearly two weeks now. Surely he should be home before long. D — don't you think?"

David drew a deep breath. "I hope and pray he will, Kirsten. But please don't worry. Trust God to bring him back safely. And please call on me when you need me."

"I will." She smiled weakly. "You're so good, David. I don't know what I'd do without you."

He came toward her and gently took her hands in his. "Some day I'll take care of you always, my dear one." Then he turned abruptly and slammed out of the house.

Kirsten watched him go. *What a fine young man,* she thought. *I only wish I could love him — the way I love Wil Patten.* . . . Then she caught herself fiercely. I must put Wil out of my mind.

120

"So you're going to marry David Poffenberger, Kirsten?" Lelo stood in the kitchen doorway. "Or do you have a choice?"

"Oh. . . ." Kirsten gave her head a fierce shake. "I'm so confused, Lelo. I don't know what to do." She stood hesitantly, then with a determined jut to her jaw, she burst out, "I don't have to decide just this minute, do I?" She laughed shakily. "Besides, my job is taking care of Papa's household. Pity poor Lelo — ruining her pretty hands peeling apples! As long as I'm needed here, I'll stay."

A satisfied smile played on Lelo's lips. "I thought you'd come to your senses. Papa would never let you go anyhow, would he?"

Kirsten moistened her dry lips. "Not for a long time, Lelo. Maybe some day — But why should I be the one to sacrifice myself?" she flared, suddenly recalling Allie's words of a year ago.

Lelo's face sagged. "But — but that would mean — "

"It means you'd take the responsibilities I've carried since I was fifteen — and which I'm still carrying now at twenty." She took the dishes into the kitchen. "It's time we get these washed up and put away and begin on the apples. The morning's half gone, and before long Peter and Andrew will want lunch."

The long day finally wheeled to a close as the sun left its smoldering fire above the distant hill and disappeared. The embers that flared briefly in the west faded to sullen gray ashes.

Peter whistled when he came in from the barns and corrals and Kirsten felt a lift in her heart. All signs of his earlier morose behavior had vanished. Although she missed Papa dreadfully, she was happy that Peter's tension had gone. Perhaps her prayers for her oldest brother were being answered and he was changing his attitude about farming. In another week or so Papa would be home, and things would return to normal. That is, if the war would end.

Would I marry David then? she asked herself as she crawled into bed beside the gently sleeping Lelo that night. She honestly didn't know.

When she awoke the next morning to a bright blue September sky, Kirsten hurried down to the kitchen to prepare breakfast. A few clouds hung overhead, and the sunny fields to the west lay swathed in yellow-green. Any minute now Peter would tromp downstairs and be off to the barns to milk the two cows and feed the horses.

After the table was set and the cornbread ready for the oven, Kirsten peered at the mantel clock. Peter should have been up half an hour ago. He'd most likely overslept. She went to the stairway and called:

"Peter? Andrew? It's time to get up. You — Lelo and Heidi — what's keeping you?"

Five minutes later Andrew padded down the stairs, yawning and wiping his sleep-fogged eyes.

"Wonder why Peter didn't wake me," he mumbled.

"Peter? He hasn't come down."

"But he must have. He sure wasn't in our room."

A sudden fear clutched at Kirsten's heart, and she looked around the dining room wildly. Suddenly she spied an envelope propped up against the kerosene lamp on the small table, and she hurriedly tore it open. The words seemed to leap out at her with the fierceness of a booming gun.

Kirsten — I'm very sorry but I couldn't help myself. You know I haven't been happy on the farm for a long time. I guess I'm letting you down, and Papa most of all, for he had trusted me to stay. But I had to do it — even if the church disapproves. I know it's what God wants of me, no matter what you may think. I'm joining General

123

McClellan's Army of the Potomac with the ambulance corps, so I won't be carrying a gun. I left David a note, telling him to help you if you need it, but you've always been so strong and dependable I know you'll get along fine without me. Andrew does a good job in the barns. God bless you all.

There was no signature. With a sharp painful breath, Kirsten leaned herself against the wall. So that's what Peter's plan was all about — why he was so cheerful and happy these past several weeks. She shook her head sadly. Dear God . . . why couldn't I stop him? Then she reread the note. No one could have stopped Peter.

With a resolute thrust to her shoulders, she made her way woodenly toward the kitchen.

11

Kirsten moved like a sleepwalker, her mind in a daze. *I should've suspected this,* she upbraided herself firmly. *I should've seen it coming. Now I feel I've let Papa down — the whole family, in fact.*

Heedless of the uneaten breakfast on the table, she grabbed her bonnet and let herself out the front door. She walked woodenly toward the rail fence that ran along the lane, crawled awkwardly over the split rails, and started up the hill that hid the farm from view on the east. The view from the hill provided a splendid vista of the countryside. Meadow grass was already turning tawny in the early September sunshine, and she panted a little as she made her way through the thick russet tufts to the top.

Looking toward the east, she shaded her eyes against the rising sun, craning her neck as though she would catch sight of Peter's thin hurrying figure on his horse, riding along the road beyond. Almost impulsively she thought of rushing to the Poffenbergers' and asking David to go after her brother and bring him back. Then sanity overtook her. She had no idea when Peter had left, or which road he had taken. Besides, Peter wouldn't wish to be dragged back. It would create more problems than it solved. He would only become more moody. This was something Peter had schemed and planned for a long time. In fact, he had insisted this was God's way for him. What right would man have to force him back against his will?

Here she was — left alone with three younger siblings to face an uncertain future. Yet always this fact was punctuated with the words: *You are dependable; you can handle it.* But this did not alter the fact that somehow she felt she had let Peter down — and what was worse, she had failed Papa. Where did all that *dependability* fit in? The word suddenly tasted bitter.

"Dear Lord," she prayed aloud. "I feel so inadequate to handle all this. Please help me."

A sudden sound behind her startled her, and she spun around. David Poffenberger, his clean, shining eyes under his wide-brimmed hat searching her agonized face, stood there.

"Kirsten," he said, taking her hands in his, "I came as soon as I found the note Peter left me. I know my place is with you at this trying time."

She pushed back her bonnet and leaned her head against his broad chest. "Oh, David. I'm so glad you're here! I don't know what I'd do without you. Papa left me in charge, and I've failed him miserably."

He stroked her dark hair gently. "No, Kirsten, you haven't. You don't have to answer to Peter's actions," he said softly. "Peter is responsible for his own decisions." Then he held her away from him and looked straight into her eyes. "Kirsten, marry me — now! I can best look after you if I'm around for good."

She drew her breath sharply. Marry David? It would solve everything. He would help her bear her trials and take over responsibilities. *But I don't love David.* The thought hit her with an impact, and she shook her head.

"No, David. Papa — the family depends on me. I can't think of marrying anyone. It's good of you to be so concerned, and I appreciate that. Perhaps some day. . . ." Her voice broke. Maybe in time she'd forget Wil Patten and fall in love with David Poffenberger.

"Oh, Kirsten — I do love you, my dear! I promise to make you happy." He bent his head and kissed her softly on the lips. Hers felt no urge to respond, and she pushed him away gently.

"Please . . . don't, David. I might be vulnerable and it's all very tempting. But my first duty is to my family."

"I — see," he said slowly, his eyes full of pain. Kirsten was sure he *didn't* see.

"Well, I'll come whenever you need help. Promise to let me know," he added.

"I will." Kirsten nodded. "At least, until Papa comes. He should be back soon."

David took her hand and they started slowly down the hill. They talked of the war and what the Sharpsburg community might expect. He said he would check often until her father returned.

"I'm glad we live off the beaten path," she said. "Our farm is secluded enough so that we're reasonably safe from marauding soldiers."

"Yes, I believe you are right. But I must make sure. See you in church Sunday?"

"Yes, David. We'll be there."

Surely Papa would be home by Sunday. He had been gone for over two weeks. As long as he was away, Kirsten must accept responsibility for Lelo, Heidi, and Andrew, and the daily chores on the farm. But, she knew Lee's Confederates were in good spirits, and morale was never higher after the North's aborted attack on Richmond.

"None but heroes are left," one Rebel soldier had written home. In little more than two months these heroes had driven the Federals from the outskirts of Richmond all the way back to fortifications around Washington. Now the Rebels were about to set foot on Union soil.

On September 4, Confederate troops began their march toward the Potomac. The invasion of Maryland had begun as they crossed the broad river, fringed with lush trees and flanked with a riot of wild flowers. In Washington the news of the Rebel crossing hit like an artillery shell as a Maryland farmer on horseback raced down Pennsylvania Avenue shouting the news.

When the small German Baptist congregation met for services on September 7, talk focused on the invasion. They knew General McClellan had marched his troops into Maryland, but no one was sure where the Confederates were headed. Uncertainties mounted. The distant boom of artillery sounded sporadically from the area of nearby Frederick, a scant 25 miles to the southeast. Possibly some troops were already engaged in battle.

Papa still hadn't returned and Kirsten was becoming increasingly worried. Was it possible he had been captured by the Confederates? The thought cut through her like a knife.

An undercurrent of deep concern swept through the service. Word of Peter's leaving to join the army had become a topic of conversation before the meeting started. After the usual morning message, the congregation remained to make some decisions.

"We are right in the path of the advancing armies," Elder Mumma said gravely. "Our lives could be in danger and we urge those of you who feel so inclined to flee."

A low murmur of voices droned over the group. Kirsten glanced around. Allie Mumma, sitting beside her, touched her arm.

"What will you do. Kirsten? Since your father and Peter are gone — "

"I promised Papa we would stay. What about you?"

Allie cocked her bright head. "My father says, as the presiding elder, he won't go either. But I have this strange feeling. . . ." Her voice trailed away.

Some families favored evacuation. The Manor Church lying nearer the Pennsylvania border, was opening its doors to the

Mumma congregation.

Daniel Miller rose to his feet. "We plan to leave some time this week. Others are welcome to join us."

When the meeting was dismissed with the benediction, Kirsten hurried out to the carriage. She was anxious to go home, for she was in no mood to discuss Peter's disappearance — or Papa's prolonged absence. She had avoided David's searching gaze in church all morning, knowing he would urge her to marry him so he could look after her.

"And I can't do that," she told herself fiercely. "Not even a marriage of convenience."

Perhaps if she had never met Wil Patten, her response might have been different.

The Webers ate their noon meal in silence. Kirsten had always joined in with Heidi's and Andrew's chatter; today she was too wrapped up in her own thoughts to listen. The thick beef stew steamed with hearty flavor but she barely tasted it.

Lelo kept eyeing her furtively and Kirsten felt like screaming for her to stop. Finally she couldn't keep quiet.

"I know you're all scared, and so am I," she flared, pushing her plateful of stew away. "We could evacuate but I promised Papa we'd be here when he got back. If we all stick together we can make it."

Andrew sniffed derisively. "I'm not afraid, Kirsten. Remember the verse that hangs over the front of the church? 'The Lord is our shepherd . . .' and we're to fear no evil for he's with us. That's what Papa would say, isn't it?"

"You're right, Andrew," Kirsten answered slowly. "Everything's sort of — hit us all at once. Peter gone — Papa still away — and now the — the armies heading our way. I guess I almost forgot about — about our Shepherd. Thank you, Andrew, for reminding us. Of course, we'll be all right."

"I'll help Lelo with the housework, Kirsten, so you and Andrew can handle the chores," Heidi added quietly. "Papa will come home soon, I'm sure."

Before Kirsten could respond, a frantic rapping sounded on the front door. Kirsten jumped up and hurried to open it. Daniel Miller stood there, his ginger-colored beard glistening with sweat and his black broad-brimmed hat pushed back.

"Kirsten, we're leaving tomorrow for a place of safety. I think it's best for you and your family to join us. You can't stay here alone!"

A shiver snaked down her back as she realized the legitimate fear that lurked in the man's face.

"Thank you, Brother Miller. But — the children and I have decided to stay. I promised Papa before he left that we'd be here when he came back."

"But — but what if the soldiers come? You could be in grave danger. Surely your father would understand — "

"We have just talked it over and decided that with God's help we'll survive," she said quietly. "We can't leave the farm, the animals, and crops. We've worked for it long and hard. Please don't urge us."

"I — we feel responsible for defenseless members of the church," he said thickly. "If anything happens to you I'd never forgive myself."

Lelo pushed herself forward, her hands on her hips. "Our place is secluded enough and God knows where it is. We — we want to wait here for Papa." *Good for Lelo,* Kirsten thought.

With a tired sigh, Miller turned and walked slowly to the hitching post. Then he turned, and with a wave of his big hat, he mounted his horse and rode away.

12

The next several days dragged by with the steady boom of cannon like distant thunder. Papa still had not returned, and Kirsten was growing more apprehensive daily.

Then on Wednesday, September 10, Andrew brought home a letter sent from Washington. He handed it silently to Kirsten who was folding laundry on the dining table.

With shaking fingers she tore open the seal. It was from Papa.

I have concluded my business successfully," he wrote. "But I have been stricken with dysentery and am not well enough to come home alone. Could you send Peter after me?"

For a moment Kirsten felt a cold hand of fear move over her spine. Papa ill! No wonder he had not been able to take the long drive home. Kirsten was sure he had picked up the dysentery sleeping in strange places or eating unfamiliar foods.

"He wants Peter to bring him back" she whispered in anguish. She steadied herself against the table, then sagged into a chair and covered her face with her hands. "Dear God, what shall we do now?"

"I'm growing up," Andrew said stoutly. stretching himself as tall as possible. "Maybe I could go — "

"No!" Kirsten shouted. "No, Andrew. You're barely eleven years old! I need you here. Lelo, I just don't know — How can we — "

"Why not ask David? Or Elder Mumma?" Lelo offered, folding a clean sheet and placing it on a stack of linens. "Maybe he'll have a suggestion."

"That's a splendid idea," Kirsten said, jumping to her feet. "I'll ride up to Mummas immediately. You and Heidi can finish putting the laundry away, then pick apples in the orchard. Some we'll sort and store in the cave for winter. Andrew, check if Betsy's new calf has come in."

While she was giving orders, Kirsten tucked the escaping ringlets back into the pins and jammed the bonnet on her head. Then she hurried out to the barn, saddled Polly, and rode down the lane.

The September air was warm and sweet, and a few cauliflower clouds hung motionless in the blue sky. Cornfields stood in straight green rows, like battalions of soldiers ready for drill.

As she rode through the West Woods past the church, Kirsten breathed deeply. She had no idea how to get Papa home, for she knew it would be no easy undertaking, with soldiers covering parts of northwest Maryland on maneuvers. That there had been fighting at Frederick she was sure, but she'd heard no details.

A collie barked as she rode into the Mumma yard and stopped before the hitching rack in front of the large house. She slid from Polly's back and hurried to the front door. At her sharp rap, Allie opened it.

"Kirsten!" she squealed, "come in. We're just getting the latest news from Frederick."

"From Frederick?"

"David Poffenberger rode in after taking a horse to the Kaltheimers. They live on the outskirts of Frederick, you know."

Kirsten followed Allie into the large, airy dining room. Elder Mumma and David Poffenberger looked up from the table where they were sipping coffee when the girls came in.

David rose to his feet. "Kirsten! Is anything wrong?" he asked, his face lined with concern.

She stood silently for a minute, then thrust out Papa's letter. "Here. I've heard from Papa. He — he is ill and wants Peter to come after him. But — "

"And of course, that's out of the question," Elder Mumma said, scanning the letter hastily. "David tells me there's been some skirmishing at Frederick. God only knows where the Confederates will strike next."

"What — what happened?" Kirsten said, seating herself in the chair David had pulled out for her, and took off her bonnet.

He sat down across from her and toyed with his empty cup. "It seems General Lee's main body of Confederates was camped around Frederick. Very few sympathizers greeted them when they marched through town. A few waved Confederate flags, but most of the townsfolk seemed indifferent. Some were even hostile. They tell me the Rebels were ragged, filthy, hungry, and many were barefooted, for Lee had issued strict orders against pillaging. Well, Monday night Jeb Stuart gave a party — a grand ball in a deserted schoolhouse at nearby Urbana, with grand ladies and bands and everything. There was dancing and merrymaking. Suddenly their polkas and quadrilles were rudely interrupted by the distant boom of artillery, then the rattle of small arms. An orderly rushed in and reported that a detachment of Federal soldiers had attacked a Confederate outpost." He paused briefly and folded his hands under his chin.

"What happened then?" Allie asked, her animated features anxious.

David sighed. "Well, when Stuart's men got there, troopers from the First Carolina Cavalry had already broken the Federal attack, and they returned to their ball. But the citizens of Frederick didn't welcome them as they'd hoped. Frederick stores closed, refusing to take Confederate money, so Lee figured he'd better move on. He decided to head for Pennsylvania"

"Pennsylvania!" Samuel Mumma burst out. "What does he want there?"

"Capture the Northern rail center at Harrisburg, I s'pose."

"But then he could control the entire North!"

"Yes, that's the idea. Except that he knows he'd have to face nearly 12,000 Federals so he decided to go after Harper's Ferry with one division. The rest were to march north. Luckily there was no real fighting at Frederick. When I arrived, all the soldiers had left."

"And what's to happen next?" Kirsten

said, anxiety edging her voice. "Peter . . . Papa. . . ."

"I'll go to Washington myself and bring your father home, Kirsten," David said without hesitating.

"But — the danger — "

"Please don't argue. Someone must go, and I'll take the back roads. They should be safe enough."

Kirsten let out her breath slowly. David was as fine a man as ever lived, and she'd never forget his kindness.

"I don't know — what to say, David," she said slowly. "I'm very grateful — more than you'll ever realize."

"You know I'd do anything for you, Kirsten."

She felt red color sweep over her face, and bent her head quickly. Then swallowing her embarrassment at his words, she said, "But what will Papa say that Peter didn't come? I must tell him myself — how I couldn't stop him. . . ."

"I'll just say that we thought it best that I come instead. I've been to Washington before and Peter hasn't."

With a stiff nod, Kirsten struggled to her feet and tied her bonnet under her chin. "You're right. How soon can you leave, David?"

"In the morning, after I've made arrangements with my family. I'm sorry I can't check on you as I'd promised, Kirsten."

Elder Mumma cleared his throat. "Someone from the church can make sure all is well. I'll see to that."

"Th-thank you," Kirsten stammered, heading for the door. "I'll never forget all this — kindness."

Allie followed Kirsten out to the porch, and grabbed her arm before she started for Polly.

"*Ach,* Kirsten, how romantic!" she cried breathlessly. "David's practically laying down his life because of you."

"It's because of Papa," Kirsten snapped. "I'm only grateful that he's willing to go after my father."

"Of course! But I still say he's doing it because of you."

Kirsten climbed on her horse, and with a wave of her hand, she nudged Polly into a fast trot as they flew down the lane.

Her thoughts roiled. Would David Poffenberger demand the right to marry her now? She shook her head as she rode across the turnpike to the church. It was all so confusing. Pausing for a moment in the churchyard, she got off her horse and pushed at the south door. With a creaking sound, it opened. Slowly she walked down the center aisle and moved into the third pew. There she leaned her arms on the pew in front of her and cradled her head on her palms.

"Dear Lord," she cried. "help me to be willing — to marry David — if this is what he wants . . . in return. . . ."

Then she looked up and the verse of Scripture on the wall seemed to leap out at her. *Der Herr Ist Mein Hirte* — The Lord Is My Shepherd. . . .

Somehow she knew that, no matter what, Christ, the great Shepherd would make a way, would lead her "beside the still waters" when the time came.

With a sudden burst of elation she hurried out to Polly. After a few minutes of hard riding the farm hove into sight beyond the hill.

13

Kirsten was up early on Thursday morning, September 11. Today David would leave for Washington to bring Papa home. She knew the trip on horseback would take two or three days, and the drive back with the wagon might well last a week or more. She couldn't expect Papa for at least ten days.

But relief that finally he would come home swept over her in waves and energized her. There was much to do.

"Today we'll scrub the house from top to bottom, and clean the stables," she told her siblings at breakfast. "Papa will find everything in order when he comes. Andrew, I'm depending on you to look after the barns. Has Betsy's calf come in yet?"

"I haven't checked this morning," the eleven-year-old towhead said, wiping up the last of his porridge with a piece of cornbread. He got up for his straw hat and left the house.

Lelo's face puckered into an unbecoming frown. "Clean the house again, Kirsten? It isn't even dirty from last week! All we do is air Papa's bedding and scrub."

"I promised Papa I'd look after things while he was gone, and I won't disappoint him," Kirsten snapped.

"It gives us something to do," Heidi added, her face pensive.

With a pout, Lelo went into the kitchen for the scrub buckets while Kirsten cleared the table. She had just wiped the last dish and hung the wet tea towel over a chair to dry when Andrew came back into the house.

"I can't find Betsy," he said. "She's not in the pasture, and her calf is due any time."

"Have you scoured the woods and the fields?"

"No. But I'm sure I'll find her."

"If you need help, let me know," Kirsten said, drying her hands on a coarse roller towel.

"Sure." With a slam of the kitchen door he was off.

Kirsten tackled the kitchen, scrubbing down shelves and wiping soot which had congealed on the whitewashed cupboard. A warm September breeze blew through the open doorway and stirred the dotted swiss curtains on the north window. I'd better take them down and wash them, she decided. She had just slipped them from the rods when Andrew burst back through the door.

"I found Betsy and her calf," he said, flipping his straw hat back over his tawny hair.

"Did you? Good." Kirsten tossed the curtains on a chair. "Where was she?"

"Up toward Daniel Millers' place, north of the West Woods. I thought she wouldn't come, but Daniel Miller's new hand helped me goad her into our road. Betsy had the purtiest little bull calf you ever saw."

"Say, that's nice," Kirsten said. "Papa will be pleased. I supposed you stabled them?"

"I sure did." He grew silent, then like water from a broken dam he began to chatter. "Hoskins told me the news — how Little Mac got to Frederick and found the rascally Rebels gone. But everybody gave him a great welcome. Shutters flew open, sashes went up, and the windows filled with ladies waving their handkerchiefs and flags. Some women came out and kissed his uniform and hugged his horse Dan. It must'a been some sight."

Kirsten laughed. "It sounds like it. Well, I'm glad his Army of the Potomac is finally on its toes."

"Yup. But them Rebels is awfully sneaky. Hoskins says to be ready for anything. That there's lots of skirmishing already, especially around Turner's Gap."

"I thought Daniel Millers had left," Kirsten said, trying to ease her fears. "What is Hoskins doing there?"

"He's sort'a looking after things, I guess." Andrew dipped a drink of fresh water from the wooden pail and started toward the door. "Well, I'd better make sure Betsy is comfortable."

"You're such a big help, Andrew," Kirsten said. "I don't know how I'd manage without you."

With a merry whistle Andrew sauntered out to the barn.

As Kirsten sudsed the kitchen curtains in a pan of soapy water, her mind went back over her conversation with Andrew. *If Peter had joined McClellan's Army of the Potomac, would he be in the middle of those skirmishes? Poor Peter. He was thrust into the cruel world far too soon. But that's what he'd wanted.* Without consciously trying, she thought of Dr. Wilshire Patten. Was his medical unit busy too? Then she scolded herself. *What he does is his concern. I'll probably never see him again.* The thought made her heart constrict with pain, and she shook herself.

What's the matter with me? It's David Poffenberger I should be thinking of — David, who has gone to bring Papa home. David, who loves me and wants to marry me. . . .

The next several days passed quickly. Keeping busy with cleaning and outdoor work, the family found less time to think about the war that simmered only a few miles away and could explode into a full-blown conflict at any moment. Even then the sound of distant artillery echoed clearly over the hills.

Sunday morning dawned with bright hot sunshine. Kirsten was in the barns helping Andrew with the milking. Betsy's fresh, creamy milk would produce more butter and cheese for their cave storehouse.

"Do you think we'll have church today?" Andrew asked as they drove the cows into the stanchions.

"Why not? It's Sunday, isn't it? 'This is the day the Lord hath made. Let us rejoice and be glad in it,' says the psalmist."

"But the sounds of war — "

"The soldiers are not fighting here, Andrew!" she said brusquely. "God has promised to be with us, hasn't he?"

An hour or two later the family arrived on the small churchyard. Waves of heat poured through the open windows of the small sanctuary as Kirsten and her sisters filed down the middle aisle into the west pews while Andrew slid into a pew at the right. The congregation was scanty, for a number of families had opted to flee to safer areas.

All morning the roar of cannon and crack of gunfire from nearby South Mountain broke into their quiet services, making it hard to concentrate. The meeting closed with special prayers for safety for the little flock.

While the battle raged on South Mountain, Stonewall Jackson had slowly and methodically positioned his artillery around the Federal garrison at Harper's Ferry. Two batteries were forced to hack a narrow road out of brush up Maryland Heights to drag four Parrott guns to the summit — a task that took 200 men wrestling with the ropes of each gun. Perhaps it was well that the citizens of Washington County only surmised, as the pious German Baptist Brethren lay down for an uneasy rest that afternoon. Kirsten, trying to cover her fears, shivered in the heat of the day as she tried to nap. The crisp curtains on the open bedroom windows hung limp and lifeless in the drafts of hot, stagnant air that blew over her.

Did I do the right thing? She asked herself over and over. *Should I have taken the children and gone with Daniel Millers to safety?* But again she remembered the trust Papa had placed in her. Had they gone, what would have happened to Betsy and her calf? She tried to shut out the noise of battle in the distance. The low, dim booming might have passed for summer thunder. Except she knew — they all knew — that these were battle sounds, a fact she couldn't wipe from her mind.

Batting the hot air over her face with a folded newspaper, Kirsten lay rigid and tense with a fear to which she wouldn't admit. *I must be strong for my siblings' sake,* she reminded herself firmly. *No matter what happens, I will be calm and cheerful. After all, the fighting was still miles away. It might never reach Sharpsburg.*

She pulled herself to her feet and walked heavily down the stairs, squaring her shoulders resolutely.

Heidi sat on the rope swing that dangled from the tall walnut tree just inside the picket fence, her bare feet trailing in the dust as she pushed herself back and forth. Maroon hollyhocks lifting creamy centers to the sun nodded over one corner of the pickets.

"Oh, Kirsten!" Heidi cried when Kirsten approached, "isn't this a perfect day for a picnic supper?"

"Picnic — ? Out under the trees?" Kirsten caught herself sharply. "I — think it's a splendid idea. We need something perfect to — to end God's holy day of rest, don't we? Come on, help me fix a batch of meat and bread sandwiches. And there's leftover dried apple pie too. We'll pretend it's a very ordinary Sunday afternoon."

As the two sisters came into the cool, dim kitchen, Lelo pattered down the stairs, her eyes tired and her face drawn.

"Oh, Kirsten, I keep hearing cannon in the distance — "

"What you hear is the roll of summer thunder," Kirsten broke in.

"And we're going to have a picnic before it rains," Heidi added whimsically.

"Picnic? Rain?" Lelo shrieked. "Are you crazy? You know very well — "

"Oh, but we *don't* know." Kirsten winked at Heidi. "What I heard was thunder. Didn't you?"

Just then Andrew came panting up the lane, his tousled hair damp with sweat.

"I just — came from a little scouting expedition — along the Sharpsburg road," he shouted as he burst through the door.

"Rebel soldiers are pouring into town — thousands of 'em. I guess this means. . . ."

Kirsten shut her ears at Andrew's words as a wave of horror shot through her, and she clutched the edge of the table, her knuckles white. She could pretend no longer. The war was on their doorstep.

14

The stillness that greeted Kirsten seemed even more sinister on Monday morning. Then she heard a far-off sound, faint and sullen like the first thunder of an approaching storm.

As she got dressed, a foreboding feeling gripped her. She hurried down the stairs in the early gray morning light, let herself out of the house, and climbed the hill.

Her dreams had been clogged all night with soldiers rushing pell-mell over Washington County, and in the midst of tramping feet Peter had crawled, trying desperately to get away. But the pounding, ever-moving feet kept him immobile, his cries for help unheeded. Kirsten was glad when morning came, and the dream had popped like a bubble. But the reality of war remained.

Now as she reached the top of the hill, she

paused to watch the sunrise. Daylight came, slow and gloomy. Splotches of green touched the brown valley below but the hill slopes beyond were gray and dull against a sickly, blue-gray sky. She turned her gaze unwillingly to the south. There, not more than two scant miles away the pastures west of Sharpsburg were dotted with white tents where troops of Confederates had settled in. Beyond, twelve miles to the southwest, she saw faint puffs of smoke as far away as Harper's Ferry, and the now familiar sense of foreboding pressed down on her until she felt stifled.

With a deep, agonizing sigh Kirsten turned away. There was no doubt about it. War was about to explode everywhere.

Her legs trembled as she started back toward the house, and a flat, bitter taste filled her mouth — a taste of fear, of apprehension. Again she thought of Peter. Where was he in all this milieu of skirmishing, and how was he coping with his chosen life? Had he already regretted his part in the army of the Potomac? And was Wil Patten serving with Little Mac?

The burdens, the fears seemed to weigh her down, so that she could hardly drag herself, and as she reached the split rail fence, she leaned her arms on the topmost rail and laid her chin on her palms. She closed her eyes as tears cut shiny paths down her cheeks.

"Dear Lord," she prayed fervently, sobs choking her voice, "God — please — *please help me* . . . I can't go on — alone!"

As a sense of peace stole over her she climbed over the fence and headed for the house. *Be still and know that I am God.* . . . The words pulsed through her like an unspoken benediction.

When she reached the house, she threw back her head with a determined jerk and hurried into the kitchen. Buckwheat cakes . . . sausages . . . she would fix a hearty breakfast. No word about the sights she had seen from the hilltop would cross her lips.

"Breakfast!" she sang out half an hour later. "Anybody for pancakes and maple syrup?"

When the family trooped down the stairs, Kirsten's plans were made. "Today," she said brightly, "after morning chores, Heidi and Andrew can play wherever you wish while I store foodstuffs for safekeeping. Lelo, you shall read to your heart's content. Let's enjoy the day, and forget that distant drumroll of thunder."

Her announcements were greeted with cries of pleasure. "Kirsten — what's gotten into you?" "You're not such a slave driver after all" — "Well, *finally*. I can read all I wish. . . ."

She shooed them out of the way after the milking and other morning chores were finished and set out ingredients for bread-making. The cave was cool and moist, and loaves of fresh bread would keep for days. She would also churn the contents of the stone cream crock into butter, and maybe cook several batches of applesauce. There was nothing like exacting, exhausting work to take her mind off her sense of impending gloom.

The spicy aroma of applesauce flavored with cinnamon floated from the kitchen by midafternoon, and Kirsten surveyed the table with a satisfied smile. Freshly baked loaves of crusty wheat bread, crocks of sweet butter, and a kettle of cooked apples stood cooling on the racks.

Samuel Mumma came by just as Kirsten was washing up her dirty pots and pans.

"I thought I'd better check how you're getting along," he said, standing in the kitchen doorway and clutching his big black hat.

"We — we're holding out well," she said, giving the last utensil a brisk swipe. "See? I've been cooking and baking so we're well supplied with food. Please don't worry about us. I promised Papa we'd be here when he gets back. That could be almost any day now."

"Perhaps. Your farm is quite secluded, you know. If it weren't for that — "

"I'd be more worried if it weren't," Kirsten cut in. "But as I said before, we'll be all right."

He picked up his hat and turned to leave. "We'll check again in a day or so," he said and left.

A few minutes later Andrew came into the kitchen and sniffed hungrily. "I could smell that good cookin' a mile away. How about a chunk of fresh bread and butter, a bowl of applesauce, and a glass of buttermilk?"

"And spoil your supper? You wouldn't do that, would you?"

"Kirsten, being lazy makes me hungry. What else would you have me do?" His blue eyes sparkled with mischief. Then they looked grave. "I thought I'd better tell you. I scouted around awhile ago and met Hoskins. He says many folks from Sharpsburg have fled south — and some have gone to Klingburg Cave. McClellan chased the Rebels out of South Mountain — especially after Corporal Mitchell stumbled upon Lee's Special Order Number 191, which spelled out Rebel plans."

"And what has that got to do with the war?"

"Don't you see? Little Mac can wipe up the Rebels in one big swoop!"

"If he's on his toes, that is. But I saw the Rebel tents this morning. The sight was awesome. They — they're awfully close, Andrew." She had decided to tell him after all.

"Yeah." He nodded. "I hope they don't find us hidden behind our hill. They're trying to latch onto Harper's Ferry again, Hoskins says."

"Andrew, please don't roam far from the farm," Kirsten said anxiously. "I don't want anything to happen to you."

"Don't worry, Kirsten. I can take care of myself."

She tried to ease her fears but they lingered. The Confederate camp — at least one flank — had settled too uncomfortably near.

Tuesday morning dawned gray and gloomy. Kirsten decided the family needed more time to sort out their feelings about the war, considering the nearness of the enemy. She would give them another day off. Betsy's calf seemed to be doing well, and she told Andrew so.

"But keep the cattle in the corral. We

don't want to lose any. Just fork down plenty of hay," she added.

"No Reb is going to make off with any of Papa's livestock, if I can help it," he snorted. "Hoskins says Samuel Poffenbergers are hiding their horses in their basement."

"In the basement!" Lelo burst out. "How in the world can they manage that?"

"I guess if you treasure something, you do all you can to protect it. They're muffling the hooves with old rugs."

Kirsten looked at the gray overhead sky and furrowed her brow. Then she set to work filling the wash boiler with water to scrub last week's wash. Anything to keep busy.

She had placed the tubs under the trees in the backyard and was filling them with hot, soapy water when Lelo and Heidi came out.

"We've had enough play and decided to help you," Heidi said, picking up a pile of soiled towels and plunged them into one of the large tubs.

"Yes, it looks like rain," Lelo added. "We'll have to hurry to get the clothes dry."

Kirsten smiled. Lelo must have caught up with her reading.

After the clothes flapped in the warm breeze, she carried more foodstuffs into the cave. Hungry soldiers meant raiding. It was best to hide it — just as Samuel Poffenbergers had hidden their horses.

The interminable day finally wheeled to a close. As gray clouds lowered, a whiplash of rain flicked against the windowpanes, and a sudden gust of wind blew through the treetops. Darkness was gathering now, and great folds of gray were lapping against lighter gray as the steady rain spattered and dripped from the eaves.

Kirsten lay in bed for a long time that night, praying for Papa and David on their way back from Washington; for Heidi, for Andrew and Lelo, and for all of Washington County. As she thought of the army bedded down so near, another shudder gripped her.

"Lord," she prayed, an uneasy fear holding her in its grip, "may the rain and darkness put an end to war plans . . . I've done all I can . . . all I know how . . . as I promised Papa."

Tomorrow, she decided, Lelo and Andrew must help her drive the livestock into the South Woods. It was the best place to hide them.

The steady beat of rain on the windows lulled her into drowsiness, and finally she rolled over and went to sleep.

15

Kirsten awoke early on Wednesday, September 17, with a suffocating sense of dread. The rain of the night had stopped but the early morning was still gray. She lit the lamp by her bed and glanced at the small clock on the dresser. Five-thirty. Almost as though the clock sent out a signal, a horrible sound of shelling shattered the air. It seemed so near that she jumped out of bed and flew to the window. In the early grayness she could see nothing.

Pulling on her clothes with stiff, shaking fingers, she hurried woodenly down the stairs and opened the front door cautiously. Still seeing nothing, she stepped out into the sweet morning air, and started for the hill. The noise of gunfire grew louder, amplified as it echoed across the hill. At first the boom of artillery began like pattering raindrops, then it came like a roll, a crash, roar, and rush — like an ocean surging upon the shore. Like the crashing of thunderbolts.

She picked up her skirts and stumbled up the hill, panting as she climbed. Her heart in her throat, she felt its frantic pounding as she surveyed the surrounding territory. Fog lay thick in the hollows, although the ridges were clear. To the east she saw a vast moving gray mass, pushing toward the Dunker Church along the Hagerstown turnpike. Rebel soldiers! As she strained her eyes in the dim light she could make out eight cannon and a dozen larger guns on the hill near the church, about two miles away.

Her lips dry, she scudded down the hill and scrambled over the fence. Her full skirts caught on a rail and she heard the sharp sound of ripping cloth.

Dear God, help us! she whispered, her lips frozen with fear. There was no time to lose. She must alert her siblings to be ready for any event. By the time she panted into the house, Andrew was standing anxiously at the dining room window, his face strained. Heidi sobbed in one corner, while Lelo stood, grim-faced and trembling, and gripped the lean of one of the dining chairs. As the roar of gunfire grew louder, Heidi's sobs intensified.

"There must be at least twenty-four

Parrott guns firing sixty rounds a minute," Andrew muttered, whirling away from the window. "But they're shooting away from us. Our hill's protecting us from view." He turned to Heidi and yelled suddenly, "Heidi, stop your bawling!" Nervously, he threw himself into a chair.

Mechanically Kirsten began breakfast preparations, trying to shut out the ominous crackle of a thousand rifles and booming thunder of cannon. What was there to say?

She groped for words. "Andrew's — right. The fighting isn't — aimed our way. We — we must eat a hearty breakfast and hurry through the chores. Then we'll drive the livestock into the South Woods. After that — " She paused.

"After that — *what*, Kirsten?" Lelo said, her big, baby-blue eyes wide with terror. Heidi's cries mounted into a wail.

Kirsten dropped the spoon with a clatter and moved toward her. "Please, little sister. Crying won't help."

"We should've gone with — with Daniel Millers!" Heidi choked out. "Then we'd be — safe."

"I promised Papa we'd wait here," Kirsten said softly, taking the quaking sturdy figure in her arms. "We've plenty of food in our cave, and we'll stay here as long as we can."

She led Heidi to a chair by the table and sat down beside her.

Heidi's sobbing had changed to a whimper, even as the sound of gunfire intensified. Soon it became a prolonged roar in the area of the church.

No one spoke. It was as though everyone was numb with horror and fear, and three people sat motionless — all but Lieselotte who continued to stand rooted behind her chair, her hands clenched. The din of battle rose to a mind-numbing pitch and the roar of infantry in the distance was beyond anything conceivable.

I must do something, Kirsten thought. Lord, what can I do — except pray? Suddenly she opened her mouth and her words bobbed like stringent bottle corks:

"'Fear thou not; for I am with thee; be not dismayed; for I am thy God: I will strengthen thee; yea, I will help thee; yea, I will uphold thee with the right hand of my righteousness.' That's from Isaiah 41, my dears. God is our strength, our refuge. We must believe that — and go on."

She struggled weakly to her feet and continued breakfast preparations. Heidi stopped crying although her sniffling continued, and Lelo came into the kitchen to help. Andrew once more took his post by the window.

With the roar of gunfire and exploding cannon constantly in their ears, the family made a pretense of eating the ham and eggs Kirsten and Lelo had prepared.

As soon as the meal was finished, Andrew slipped out toward the barns. Kirsten turned to her sisters.

"Girls, there's work to be done, war or no war. Heidi, you take care of the breakfast things while Lelo helps Andrew and me with the chores. Come on, girls. Your brother doesn't let fear hold him back!"

"Yes, but he's a boy," Heidi sputtered. "Boys are s'posed to be braver than girls!"

Without another word, Kirsten picked up two milk pails and set out for the barns. She heard Lelo's heavy breathing behind her. The acrid smell of gunpowder permeated the stiff morning breeze with the constant scream of shot in their ears as bullets sprayed blue against gray. Andrew had already let the cows into the barn and was forking down hay into the mangers.

Silently the two girls sat down to milk the cows while Andrew fed the pigs and calves.

As Kirsten carried the two pails of foaming milk toward the house, she glanced toward the northeast. A heavy pall of gunsmoke hung in the air and the sulfuric smell of powder seemed to grow even stronger. A blistering volley of shots erupted from beyond the church, answered by a thundering roar as canister returned fire.

Hurrying into the kitchen, Kirsten began to strain the milk into huge stone crocks. Heidi had finished the dishes and was hanging up the tea towel. She was still sniffling.

"We'll go out to the cave now, won't we?" she asked in a quivery voice.

"As soon as we drive the cattle into the woods. I'm almost done straining the milk. Now we can — "

The slam of the screendoor interrupted her and she looked up to see Lelo standing in the doorway, her face white.

"Lelo — has anything happened?" Kirsten asked, her heart hammering with new fear. "Andrew?"

Lelo gripped the sides of the door. "After I let the cows out, I came back — into the barn. There I saw — I saw. . . ."

"Quick! What did you see, Lelo?" Kirsten yelled, shaking her sister impatiently.

"Martin — Martin Druse. He — he's been wounded. He — he just staggered into the barn and — and collapsed on the — the straw. Oh, Kirsten — he's been shot!"

For a moment Kirsten stared at Lelo, then she pressed her lips into a tight line. "Come on," she ordered, pushing her way through the doorway and heading for the barn. "We must bring him into the house."

Lelo scrambled to keep up with Kirsten's fast stride. "But he's our — enemy," Lelo ventured. "Do you think we should — "

"He's hurt, isn't he?" Kirsten snapped. "Since when do Baptist Brethren ask who their brother is?"

She rushed into the barn and ran toward the soldier who had fallen onto a pile of straw. His face was contorted with pain and a sticky red wetness seeped through the chest of the dirty gray uniform. Kneeling down, Kirsten felt his pulse. It was weak and irregular.

"Quick, Lelo!" she cried urgently. "Help me get him into the house and into Papa's bed."

Lelo and Kirsten struggled to get the wounded young man on his feet, and with his dead weight between them, they inched toward the house. He bore no resemblance to the jaunty young man they had met last year at Daniel Millers'. The noise of exploding canister and screeching, ear-splitting shells whistled to their right. With a cry, Lelo dropped her end of the burden. Kirsten grabbed the man quickly, her arms almost torn from her sockets as she literally dragged him up the brick-paved path to the door of the house. His groans increased.

Lelo had run ahead and held the door open as Kirsten pulled her burden into the front hall.

"Run ahead and fold back Papa's sheets," Kirsten ordered. "Hurry! Don't stand there like a fool — This man needs help!"

Heaving with all her might, she maneuvered Druse's body onto the edge of the bed. Lelo had finally composed herself and picked up the filthy, dirt-encrusted legs, laying them onto the bed.

"Get into the kitchen and heat some water," Kirsten said sharply, feeling the young man's pulse again. Had it grown weaker? "And bring some old sheets for bandages!" Lelo stood and watched indecisively. "Hurry! What's keeping you?"

After the girl had left, Kirsten unbuttoned the blood-soaked shirt and pulled it as gently as she could from his body. The hideous, gaping shoulder wound near his chest repulsed her. It spelled death unless he received help right away. Quickly she jerked the tattered boots from calloused feet. As gently as she could, she turned him to one side and drew off the dirty trousers.

Lelo brought a pan of hot water and some towels, and set them on the bedside table. The moans were growing fainter. After checking his pulse, Kirsten wrung out a cloth and began to sponge the bloody chest carefully. With each pat of her wet rag, fresh blood spurted from the wound.

Lelo clutched her arm in fear. "Kirsten . . . do you think — he's going to — "

"I don't know!" Kirsten flared. "He's wounded badly, and he's in shock. All we can do is take care of him and pray that he'll make it. Get some more blankets from the closet. We've got to keep him warm."

Heidi stood in the doorway, her face drawn at the sight. "When are we going into the cave, Kirsten?" Her tone was whining.

"Oh, for heaven's sake, Heidi — can't you see what's happened? We've got a wounded Rebel in Papa's bed, who isn't going to die if I can help it," Kirsten said fiercely. Then in a gentler voice she added, "I'm sorry for yelling, Heidi. I'll stay here. If you and Lelo want to go to the cave — "

"Oh, Kirsten! It's just that I'm so s-scared. . . ."

"Sure, I know, honey. We all are."

Lelo marched into the room, carrying an armful of blankets with a determined step. "I'm staying too, Kirsten. Martin — isn't some stranger. He's someone we know — someone we — I care about very much!" Her blue eyes grew soft. "I don't know what

167

got into me out there. I guess I just — just panicked."

Kirsten looked up from her sponging with a wan smile. "I understand. We're all on edge today. I'm just glad Papa isn't home. Here, let's bandage Martin's chest and get him into one of Papa's clean night-shirts."

After the soldier had been bandaged and dressed, Lelo sat down by the bed and stroked the matted auburn curls which had fallen over his sweaty forehead. His moans had simmered to a low wheezing sound, and again Kirsten checked his pulse. Then she placed a hand on his forehead. It was growing uncomfortably warm.

Turning to Heidi, she said, "Get cold water from the spring and place cool compresses on his brow. We've got to hold the fever down." The sound of shooting continued in the background with the constant whine of bullets and shattering cannon.

Picking up the dirty gray shirt and trousers, Kirsten carried them into the kitchen and turned them over in her hands. They were good for nothing but rags.

Andrew came into the door and saw her fingering the soldier's clothes. "Kirsten!" he said. "What's that?"

Kirsten sighed. "These rags belong to

Martin Druse. He must've wandered away in a daze after he was wounded and stumbled into our barn where Lelo found him. We got him into Papa's bed and have just cleaned him up."

"Is he hurt bad?"

"I'm not sure, but the wound seems quite near the heart. It's bleeding which means the bullet must still be lodged somewhere in his chest."

"What are you going to do about it? Or about him?"

"I don't know, Andrew. All I know is that he needs help. We'll do all we can."

Andrew looked around furtively. "How about the livestock? We'd better move it pretty quick. If Martin Druse has wandered this way, God only knows who else may find us."

"You're right. Of course, he knew where we lived. Let me tell Lelo."

Kirsten tiptoed to the bedroom door. Lelo sat by the bed, gently pressing a moist cloth on Martin Druse's gray, haggard face. She looked up at Kirsten's step in the doorway.

"I'll stay right here, Kirsten," she said in a low voice. "I don't care if he is a Rebel. Once I cared about him — very much. I think — I still do."

"I know, Lelo. You just stay here while

Andrew and I drive the animals into the woods. Heidi can keep you supplied with cool water."

Then she followed Andrew out the door and toward the barns. Smoke rolled like low-hanging clouds above the trees as the cannonading continued and death screamed overhead. Dear God, Kirsten thought, will this fighting never end?

Pushing, shoving, leading — Kirsten and Andrew maneuvered the animals toward the woods. Since Papa had taken the team of work horses and Peter his roan, the only horses left on the farm were Polly and Pet. In a matter of minutes the two horses were tethered to a pair of staunch oaks near a small winding creek.

"I'll bring them fodder every day," Andrew said, and Kirsten knew he would. He had grown up almost overnight since Peter was gone. She didn't know what she'd do without him.

In the near distance the shelling continued, sometimes abating for several minutes, then a fresh volley screamed that tore huge craters in the fields as the roar of canister and whine of bullets accelerated.

Before she set out for the house, Kirsten hurried up the hill. Her glance strayed toward the east. To her horror she saw flames leaping high into the air just northeast of the church where the Mumma farm had once stood, and her heart sank. The soldiers were not satisfied with killing; now they were burning farms!

Back in the house, she found Lelo faithfully bathing Martin Druse's gray face. She picked up a limp hand and checked his pulse. There seemed to be no throb at all, then very faintly she found an unsteady beat in one wrist.

He moaned and began to thrash wildly, his arms flailing. Kirsten tried to hold him down by force.

"How long has he been like this, Lelo?" she asked anxiously.

"He just started. Mostly he just moans and at times he gasps. I just don't know what to do, Kirsten!"

"You're doing fine, Lelo. But I think he's developing a fever, which is why he's tossing this way."

Lelo turned stricken eyes to Kirsten. "What does this mean?"

"It means — he may have pneumonia, and as long as the bullet is embedded in his chest, he'll probably grow worse. He could die."

"Isn't there anything you can do?" Lelo's voice was anguished.

"Nothing — but pray. I'm sure you've done plenty of that already."

She left the room and went into the kitchen. Was there nothing she could do to help? Food. She remembered the beef stock that simmered in the pot over the fireplace. Perhaps a bit of broth. It would give him strength so his body could fight infection.

Dipping a small amount into a cup, she took it into the bedroom. The moaning and tossing continued.

"Let's see if he'll drink this broth. Can you hold him up while I try to spoon it into his mouth?"

Lelo nodded, and slipped her arms around the thin shoulders and pulled him to a semi-upright position. He screamed with pain, and with an agonized look, she laid him down on the bed again.

"It won't work, Kirsten! He's hurt too badly."

With a wary nod, Kirsten set the cup on the dresser and pulled the covers around him. Then she carried the cup back into the kitchen.

Just then Andrew burst into the house, his hair tousled and askew. "Guess what. I scouted around and — "

"You — *what?*" Kirsten said sharply. "Andrew — "

172

"No — wait, Kirsten. I know my way around. I skirted the battle area. They're fighting in Daniel Miller's cornfield, and the shooting there is fierce. The Rebels are settled around the West Woods while the Yankees have been pushing from the east. They're using the *pike* as the battleground, Kirsten. I — I sneaked close to General Hood's post and overheard him and General Mansfield talking."

Kirsten grew weak at his news. "Andrew. . . . What did you learn?" she choked out finally.

"The Rebels have straddled the Hagerstown pike and marched from one patch of woods through Millers' field into the West Woods. Fightin' Joe Hooker's men came bowling down the pike against Lee's line, and the cornfield turned into an awful holocaust. Rifle and artillery fire slashed the ripe corn, knocking men down in rows! Then Hood's Texans pushed around the church and sent Hooker's men reeling back through the cornfield. Mansfield said its fire was like a scythe running through their line! Then the Yanks barreled into the Miller barnyard with a six-gun battalion that tore the charging Texans apart. They seesawed back and forth between the East Woods and West Woods across that neat 40-acre corn patch and finally wound up fighting by the rail fence along the pike. I guess the Rebs are still hanging on by a thread. The shootin's stopped there for now. He said the carnage was awful."

"How horrible!" Kirsten gasped.

"It seems like the two hours of fighting was just to litter the cornfield with dead and wounded. But I guess the West Woods is still full of Rebels."

Kirsten took a deep breath. "Andrew, I don't want you to wander around there any more! It's much too dangerous." Her voice was firm.

"Aw, Kirsten. I learn a lot this way. Besides, no one pays attention to a country boy. A couple of soldiers saw me and asked what I was doing there. I pretended not to understand English and answered them in German!" He chuckled as though it was some huge joke.

Kirsten frowned. "Oh, Andrew — don't take chances! I'd feel better if you — "

"Kirsten, come quick!" Lelo stood in the dining room doorway and called frantically.

Jumping up, Kirsten rushed toward the bedroom. "What is it, Lelo?"

The Rebel was turning and tossing, his sharp moans like slashes of a knife. Kirsten grabbed one flailing hand and gripped it tightly. His pulse was racing furiously, and his face was flushed and pouring wet with sweat.

"We must sponge his whole body with cool water," Kirsten said, "to bring down the fever!"

With the squeamish Lelo's help, Kirsten slipped off the damp nightshirt and sponged off the sweaty naked body. The percussive sounds of Parrott shells seemed to grow louder in the background. Kirsten tried to shut her mind to everything but saving Martin Druse's life.

16

For two hours Kirsten and Lelo worked over Martin Druse, trying to cool his feverish body and relieve his agitation. It was a constant battle. Heidi was kept busy bringing cold water from the spring in the cave.

As Martin finally began to relax, Kirsten leaned back against the wall, exhausted.

"Surely God was with us," she said with a deep sigh. "I don't know how else he could have made it."

"That bullet's got to be removed," Lelo said jadedly, holding Martin's thin palm in one hand and batting the warm air with a folded newspaper with the other.

"I know, Lelo. But without a doctor — "

"I suppose Dr. Biggs from Sharpsburg — "

"We can't risk going into a town full of Rebel soldiers! Besides, he's probably joined the Union army medical corps.

Lelo inhaled sharply, and her eyelids

drooped. "Then all we can do is pray that somehow, someone will be available to do the job."

Kirsten pulled herself wearily to her feet. "I wonder where Andrew is. Come to think of it, he hasn't been in for the last two hours." Shaking her head, she added, "I don't know what to do with that boy. He roams all over the area. I've ordered him to stay home but he's so independent. As if I didn't have enough worries. . . ."

She started toward the dining room as she spoke and glanced at the clock on the mantel. It was after two-thirty. The sound of shelling seemed to have moved toward the south. Now and then there was a lull in the cannonading. Or had their ears become accustomed to the rumble of artillery, the staccato of rifle fire? Each time another explosion shattered the air she shuddered. Hidden behind their hill, they could see nothing but faint smoke that hovered like a haze over the landscape.

Heidi came in with a pail of fresh water. Although she seemed more resigned to the intolerable situation, the look of fright never quite left her face.

"When I'm in the cave," she said, "I can hardly hear a thing. Maybe we should sleep there tonight."

Kirsten went to the window and pushed the curtain aside. "Without a bed?" she said lightly.

"Oh. I've already dragged in some blankets and fixed up a pallet. It's quite cool and cozy.

"And so, my little cave-dweller, you have permission to go back to your refuge," Kirsten said gently.

Suddenly Andrew swung around the bend of the hill, and Kirsten saw the animation on his face. He slammed into the house and flung his straw hat on the table. A mysterious light gleamed in his eyes. He stood in front of Kirsten, excitement making him fidgety.

"Kirsten — I know you said to stay around, but I just had to go. Do you know something? Dr. Patten's at Daniel Miller's place, patching up the wounded!"

His abrupt announcement sent blood rushing to her face. "Andrew — what are you saying?" She'd tried hard to forget Wil, and in all the excitement she had barely thought of him all day. Grabbing Andrew's shoulders, she shook him. "Did he see you? What's happening out there?"

"The fighting's moved farther south, but the wounded are brought in by ambulances about as fast as you could blink your eyes.

No, he was too busy to notice me."

"Did you see Peter? Was he with the ambulances?"

Andrew shook his head. "No. But at least four or five surgeons are operating and amputating. . . ."

"Operating! I suppose they have medications?"

"I didn't stop to ask. They were all so busy. It looked gruesome and I left as soon as I could. But the Rebels burned the Mumma farm. Their house is just ashes and smoke now."

Kirsten let out her breath slowly, remembering what Allie had said not long ago about how much she loved their place. Poor Allie! Now they would probably never live there again.

"I trust the Mummas are safe. But their farm was right in the battle zone, so near the church. Did you notice if the church was shelled?" she asked.

"Just some big shell holes. But it's still standing. It'll prob'ly be used as a hospital. All big places seem to be. I didn't go near it." He started for the door.

"Thank God, you didn't." She heard him go out. Closing the west shutters against the hot afternoon air, Kirsten went back into the bedroom. Lelo was still keeping her quiet vigil at Martin's bedside. He had begun to stir restlessly again. Would the struggle begin all over, trying to cool down his fevered body and calming him?

Her thoughts roiled. The man needed help, for as long as the bullet remained in his chest, fever would rage. Andrew had said there were doctors at the Miller farm, and doctors dug out bullets and poured in medication. But Martin Druse was a Rebel. No loyal Union surgeon would give him the time of day. Would Dr. Wilshire Patten leave his post because she asked him as a favor? *I have ignored his letters, and avoided him for months*, she told herself. *Why should he?*

She began to pace back and forth, her mind in a whirl. *Wil Patten was a physician, and Martin Druse needed medical care. But Martin was the enemy. I couldn't ask Wil. Yet Martin needs help* . . . the thoughts pounded through her mind like a broken shingle flapping in the wind. Wil Patten has said he loves you . . . perhaps he'll do it for you . . . but you can't expect him to leave his post . . . besides, what would he think if he knew you were harboring a Rebel soldier?

"Kirsten, stop that pacing!" Lelo burst out irritably. "You're getting on my nerves!"

With a shake of her head, Kirsten left the room. She didn't know what to do. Martin

Druse was dying and he needed help. Did she dare ask to save his life?

She went back to the dining room and knelt down by the south window, leaning her elbows on the open window sill. A horrible explosive sound shrieked across the hill and she saw a churning cloud rise toward the sky. Most likely a caisson or ammunition wagon had blown up. The prolonged roar of gunfire had increased again. For a long time she remained on her knees, praying and fighting a battle of her own.

Why did life's problems fall on her shoulders? Why did God require so much of her? Decisions had bombarded her for weeks, and she could find no easy answers.

She got up and went back into the bedroom. Lelo was crying softly as she pressed Martin's limp hands to her lips. Kirsten thought his face looked more deathly gray than ever, and his moans grew more pronounced. She changed the dressing on his chest. It had soaked into a gummy, dark red splotch, glued to the bandage. Shaking her head, she chewed her lips thoughtfully. What should she do? There was nothing left.

At 5:30 the sounds of fighting had grown dimmer, and there seemed to be a lull in the battle. Perhaps the fighting was dying down.

She checked Martin's pulse once more. It

was so thin she barely found it. Suddenly her mind was made up. She turned to Lelo with a sigh.

"I'll help Andrew with the chores. After dark, Andrew and I will go to Millers' farm for Dr. Patten. Somehow we'll find help for Martin. Keep sponging his face and praying. You and Heidi will stay home — alone."

With a smothered cry, Lelo nodded. "Bless you, Kirsten. I'll pray help won't come too late."

Kirsten hurried out of the house with the milk pails and joined Andrew who was already feeding the stock in the woods.

The sun was beginning to lower in the west, and ragged clouds blotted out patches of lingering brightness. In the east for an hour or two there had been only the distant muttering of musketry from the flanks. Kirsten prayed for a quick darkness that would put an end to the slaughter and provide safe passage behind enemy lines.

After tending the livestock, she prepared a light supper. Lelo refused to leave Martin's bedside. He lay gaunt and haggard, and his breathing had grown more shallow and labored. Kirsten lit the lamp and groped for his pulse once more. She held the thin wrist for a long time before she detected a faint beat.

Placing a hand on Lelo's shoulders she said softly, "Stay right here. We'll be back as soon as we can."

"I won't leave him for a minute. Please hurry!"

Andrew was waiting in the kitchen with an unlit lantern. Kirsten stopped at the back door on her way out and turned to Heidi who was bending over the dishpan. Her usual merry face was drawn.

"I wish you'd stay here, Kirsten," she said sadly. "It's scary to be all alone with only Lelo and the dying Rebel in there!"

"You'll be fine, Heidi. Keep repeating the verse from Psalm 23: 'He leadeth me beside the still waters. He restoreth my soul.' God has kept us thus far."

Then she motioned to Andrew and the two set out in the deepening twilight. Only a random shot echoed over the hill now and then as they struck due north from the farm, across the rolling terrain. Andrew walked ahead, his footsteps noiseless in the grassy turf. He knew every inch of the land and Kirsten followed blindly.

They skirted the woods that lay north-westerly from the church. Only a faint glow from the pickets' fire stabbed through the growing darkness.

After half an hour's walk she could make

out the dark blobs of the Miller farmstead. Dim lights blinked in the barns, and everywhere she could hear moans and screams of the wounded and smell the odor of death.

Andrew paused to light the lantern, for as the bombardment had ceased, the quiet that fell over the countryside was startling. He marched ahead and made his way through the wicker gate straight to the wide porch. Here four tables had been rigged up, made of doors ripped from the house. On each lay a wounded soldier under chloroform. By the light of glimmering lanterns, surgeons worked over the sick, muttering to each other as scalpels flashed and crunched through mortifying flesh. Indoors, candles flickered in all possible places, and lanterns hanging everywhere gave off an eerie yellow light.

Kirsten peered anxiously at the surgeons who were busy with their gruesome tasks of caring for the wounded. Among the surgeons and a dozen or more aides flitted a tall, spare woman, her black hair parted in the middle, strands escaping from a braided chignon. She carried basins of water, and bent over operating tables. Once Kirsten overheard a doctor call out, "Over here, Clara."

She recalled hearing about Clara Barton,

who had followed Union troops as a field nurse. No doubt, she was helping the medical teams.

"Wait for me here, Andrew," Kirsten whispered, and threaded her way among the aides and doctors. Just then she spied Wilshire Patten bending over a soldier whose cries of pain slashed through her like a knife. A heavy canvas apron covered his uniform, now spattered and gummy with blood. She tried to read his face in the dim lantern light. The rich dark hair had tumbled over his broad forehead, and the frown that puckered his brow was more pronounced than ever. He looked weary and worn, and her heart ached for him.

As soon as he had finished with the patient on his table, Kirsten pushed her way toward him. He glanced up and saw her, and a look of pain and anger flashed in the deep blue eyes as a frown drew down the corners of his mustache.

"Kirsten! What are you doing here?" he growled. "This is no place for you."

"Oh, Wil!" she cried. "A — a wounded soldier wandered into our barn and we took him in. He has a bullet in his chest, and he'll die if it isn't removed."

"Just what did you expect me to do?"

"If you could come just long enough — "

185

"Are you more anxious for me or for the soldier?" His tone was bitter. "At least, I'll give you credit as a pacifist in doing your bit for the Union effort."

"Martin isn't a Union soldier," she burst out, "just — " she caught herself.

"You're harboring a — a *Rebel?*" he spat out the words. "If you think for one minute that I'll leave my duty to the Union — "

"Oh, Wil, he — he's a boy from Washington County — someone we know. We couldn't turn him out! The bullet — "

The pain in his eyes deepened. He came toward her and gripped her shoulders so hard they hurt. "Just give the goon some whiskey and let him go — that is, if the pious, Baptist Brethren have whiskey!" He pushed her back from him roughly. "Now let me get back to my work." He spun around and beckoned to one of the orderlies. "Next patient, please!"

Kirsten drew back, stunned. He had literally turned his back on her — the young man who had declared his undying love! Crestfallen and with a dull ache in her heart, she turned away. The moans and screams, the rushing and pushing went on as before. The odor of chloroform and cloying smells of wounds and raw flesh all around sickened her.

As she started desolately down the porch she felt a gentle tap on her shoulder. Looking up, she saw Clara Barton, her compassionate face soft in the lantern light.

"I couldn't help overhearing what you said to Captain Patten," she said. "He's one of our best surgeons and he's been under gruelling routine all day. I hope you'll forgive him."

Kirsten let out a deep sigh. "I guess I counted on — on our past friendship. . . ."

"Miss — I've been here since daybreak. You've no idea what it's been like. The whole barn is crammed with wounded, as well as the house. All I've done is wash wounds in this heat that has dried tongues and parched lips to bleeding. Roaring cannons have jarred and rolled the tables until the aides could scarcely keep the injured from sliding off during surgery! I've cooked gruel, brought out food and water, bathed faces, taken messages. . . . It's been hellish! Why I even removed a musket ball — "

"How did you do it?" Kirsten cut in eagerly. "If only I could — "

"Come with me." Clara took her arm and led her to one end of the porch. From a white enameled pan she picked up a pair of forceps and a knife. "Here. Cut away just enough flesh so you can reach the bullet, then pull it out gently with these tongs. Here's an opium pill." She fumbled in an apron pocket. "It will ease the pain. Now hurry — before your patient dies!"

"Do you think — I could do it?" Kirsten asked, her lips suddenly dry.

"If I could do it, so can you."

Kirsten grabbed the dark blue sleeve. "Have you — have you seen my brother Peter bringing in wounded with the ambulance? He's rather thin and dark — "

"Peter? I've been too busy to pay attention, but it's possible. Now scoot!"

Grabbing the instruments almost greedily, Kirsten pocketed them in her apron and hurried back to find Andrew. He leaned against a pillar of the porch where she had left him.

"Come on, Andrew. Let's hurry home."

Making their way down the dark path across the yard, they soon left the hospital and the groans and cries behind. Stars, pale and reluctant, hung in the black-sheeted sky above, almost friendly in this war-torn world.

When they neared the West Woods, Andrew blew out the lantern. "We'd better take it easy past the enemy camp. Just step carefully."

In her hurry to reach home with her

precious cargo, Kirsten stumbled over a bush in the darkness and the instruments clattered in her apron pocket.

"Halt! Who goes there?" the shrill voice of a Rebel picket called out.

Andrew gripped her arm fiercely and laid his fingers over her lips, then he shoved her down behind the bush. Kirsten's heart hammered so loud she thought surely the picket must hear it.

The two pickets swung their lanterns into a wide yellow arc. Then one of them gave a low chuckle.

"Well, Tom. I guess you're hungry for another drink o' milk. Remember, the cow we found this mornin'?" he drawled. "That was mighty fine fresh milk. I think you jest done heard another Molly Perkins cow."

After the lantern arc swung back toward the rim of trees, Andrew touched Kirsten's arm.

"Real quiet now, sis. We'd better get back home if you're gonna remove that bullet!"

17

As Kirsten and Andrew burst through the front door, Lelo jumped up and ran to meet them.

"Did you get a doctor? Is Wil Patten coming?"

With a sigh, Kirsten pushed her sister back into the chair. "No. Everyone was — so busy, taking care of the wounded. There was nothing — "

"You mean — you didn't find help?" Lelo shrieked. "But you said — "

"I know. But I did bring — this." Kirsten drew the instruments from her pocket. "Clara Barton was there, and she told me how to do it. She — "

"*You* — Kirsten? You're not a doctor!"

Kirsten shrugged her shoulders. "We haven't much choice, do we? Miss Barton said if she could do it, so could I."

She walked up to Martin, and suddenly

she noticed his eyes were open. They seemed to follow her around the room. At least, he was no longer in shock — and that was in their favor. Feeling his pulse, she drew a sigh of relief. It was somewhat stronger than earlier.

"Martin — " Kirsten touched his arm gently. "Martin, the bullet in your chest must come out. I've tried to get help, but there's so much carnage . . . so many wounded, and the doctors are all busy. I — I'll try to take it out myself. But before we do, I must warn you that you may — you may die."

He nodded faintly, and a feeble groan escaped his shaking lips. "I — I know."

She paused to moisten her dry lips with her tongue and went on. "Martin, I want to tell you — that Jesus Christ took away our sin when he died on the cross. If we accept his salvation, we needn't fear death, for he took our place. God loves us so much. He says we'll have 'everlasting life,' and that 'whosoever will may come.' Do you believe this?"

Martin struggled to speak, his voice hoarse. "I — my mother taught me this — as a child. I — I'm not af-afraid to — die . . . Le-lo, I . . . love . . . you. . . ."

Kirsten looked at Lelo, whose large blue

eyes were filled with tears, then left the room for fresh bandages and a basin of warm water. She was about to attempt the formidable task of removing Martin's bullet.

God-help-me! she prayed, her words agonized syllables. *I don't want to send this young man to his death.* . . . Oh, why was she sandbagged with so many grave decisions?

The warm air of the day had cooled to a pleasant breeze which blew in through the open window, and Kirsten breathed deeply. This would make her job easier.

"Bring the lamp, Lelo, and hold it so I can see."

After a few choking gasps, Martin had swallowed the water with the opium pill. Kirsten removed the bandage from the chest and washed the wound carefully with warm, soapy water. The bleeding had stopped and blood had congealed around the wound. Drawing another deep breath, she picked up the knife. *Cut away a bit of flesh,* Miss Barton had said, *and probe for the bullet.* She waited until Martin grew drowsy and had lapsed into a quiet sleep. Then she patted the wound with cotton once more, and eyed the raw aperture in the strong-walled chest. Musket balls sometimes made lacerated wounds, but this one looked quite clean. Instinctively she washed the instruments in the hot water to remove all foreign matter.

With a quick prayer for guidance, Kirsten bent closer and touched the wound. "Hold the lamp more to the right," she ordered, and Lelo positioned it properly. After a sharp intake of breath, Kirsten cut a small area from the opening. Blood spurted instantly, and she sopped it up with a wad of lint. Then she laid the knife into the pan of water with a clatter and picked up the forceps.

Probing gently, she eased the tips of the tongs into the gash. Blood throbbed and pulsed from the opening. *I'll have to work quickly,* she reminded herself grimly, *or the blood will flow too fast to stanch.* Biting her lower lip and flipping back the escaping tendrils from her bun, she pushed the tip of the tongs in swiftly. Ah, there was the minié ball! It was near the surface, and she could feel it easily with the forceps. Grasping it firmly, she drew it out with one flick and dropped it into the basin with a clinking sound.

Quickly she grabbed an old towel to stanch the flow of blood, packing wadded-up dressing directly into the wound, and whirled away from the bed.

"Now I'm going to run to the cave for some blackberry wine. Keep a close watch on him, Lelo," she said. "If he starts to toss, hold him down. I'll be back directly."

Stopping for the lantern, she lit it and rushed out into the cool night air. The night was breathless and still, and only the faint hoot of an owl in the woods, and an occasional hissing sound from the tree branches in front of the house marred the stillness. Now and then she heard a single shot in the battle area.

The beams from the lantern stabbed the dark path ahead with circles of light. Kirsten had hardly stopped to think of Andrew, but the pale, yellow square of light from his upper window assured her that he had gone upstairs. She stooped at the cave entrance and stepped in cautiously. On the pallet at one side, Heidi's chest moved in slow, even breathing. Poor child, Kirsten thought, it's all been so hard on her.

Groping on one end of the shelves, she found a jar of blackberry wine and carried it quickly into the house.

Give the goon some whiskey, Wil had said. He was right. They had no whiskey, but wine which was used as medicine would have to do.

Back in the house, she looked at Lelo, who nodded wearily from her bedside vigil. Martin was still sleeping quietly. She removed the packing and sopped up the blood that oozed from the wound. Then she poured in a tablespoon of wine, and strapped a bandage across the entire chest.

Lelo's head sagged with weariness. The young girl had not left Martin's side all day and far into the night, and she was exhausted. Going to the linen cupboard, Kirsten brought back several blankets. She spread them on the floor and tossed a pillow on one end.

"Here, Lelo," she ordered crisply, "I want you to lie down and sleep."

"I can't leave Martin," Lelo said with a firm shake of her head.

"You're worn out, sister. I'll sit with him while you sleep. You've got to get some rest."

Reluctantly Lelo got up from her chair, slipped off her boots, and stretched out on the blankets without another word.

Picking up Martin's hand, Kirsten felt his pulse. It was weak but steady and his breathing shallow though more regular than it had been all day. All he needed now was rest.

She watched the rise and fall of his chest for some time. It was regular. Blood oozed only sporadically from the wound to soak the dressing, and she smiled wanly. By God's grace she had succeeded in the difficult job.

Leaning back in her chair, Kirsten closed

her eyes. She was tired, so tired, but she must stay alert and watch her "patient." It was strange to think of someone else in Papa's bed. Papa! She'd hardly had time to think of him all day. Perhaps it was just as well that he was gone. If only she knew what had happened to Peter. Was it her brother who had helped bring the wounded to the hospital at the Miller farm?

Because of the heavy fighting no one from the church had come by to check, as Elder Mumma had promised. And God only knew what had happened to the Mummas since their farm was burned.

The thought she had tried to push away all night surfaced cruelly. From Wil Patten's seething anger when he had rudely brushed her aside and ordered her away, it was obvious that he had stopped caring for her. The pain of that fact seared her heart like a branding iron. That should make it easier to forget him. Yet deep down she wasn't sure she ever could.

Weariness draped over her like a soft gray cloak and she tried to stifle a yawn. She opened her eyes and looked at the sick man again. He was so quiet. Was he still unconscious from the effects of the opium? Or was he —

Again she checked his pulse. It actually

seemed stronger. With a tired smile she closed her eyes.

When Kirsten awoke, the morning sun streamed through the east windows. The dead stillness seemed almost more sinister than the distant rumble of artillery of the day before. Startled, she jumped up and checked Martin's pulse. It was regular and steady. He was sleeping naturally, and she fell down on her knees and thanked God.

Shaking Lelo's shoulder, Kirsten said gently, "It's time to get up. You'd better sit with Martin while I help Andrew with the chores."

Lelo rubbed her eyes sleepily. "Martin?"

"I think he'll be fine. He's sleeping normally."

"Thank God!"

Kirsten went into the kitchen and washed her face, and picked up her bonnet. Andrew came downstairs and yawned noisily.

"It's awful quiet, isn't it?" he muttered.

"I wonder what it means. Has the fighting stopped? Or will it begin again?"

The quiet that fell over the countryside was startling, and the stillness after the screaming day of strained nerves — the not knowing what would happen next — pressed down on her.

When she and Andrew went outdoors,

they heard the distant sound of thunder — ambulances rumbling down the road from the battlefield, and commissary wagons heading southwest on the narrow lane beyond the South Woods. Kirsten and Andrew watched from the fringe of trees.

Then a long line of soldiers were passing, their butternut uniforms dust-covered and sodden with dirt and sweat. It seemed as though there were thousands of them, bearded, dirty, their guns slung over their shoulders. Artillery rolled past — Parrott guns and canvas-covered commissary wagons that rocked and jolted along the deep ruts. The Rebel army was moving out.

With a half-fearful sense of relief, Kirsten followed Andrew back into the woods and began their chores.

Later, fixing breakfast in the kitchen. Kirsten breathed a sigh of thankfulness. Although the fighting was ended, she knew the aftermath of death and destruction remained.

Heidi wandered in from the cave, her hair tousled from sleep and her eyes bleary. "I didn't hear any shooting all night," she said, "because I slept in the cave."

"You didn't hear it," Kirsten said, "because the fighting's stopped. And Martin's better. Now you can help me fix — "

At that moment she saw several blue-coated army officers riding around the bend, and her heart raced. Had they heard about Martin Druse, the Rebel? He must be gotten away quickly or be captured as a prisoner.

She ran into the bedroom and jerked the sick man into a sitting position.

"Can you get up?" she babbled, her words coming in a rush. "Union officers are coming and we've got to get you out of here! Lelo, you and Heidi must somehow get him into the cave. Hurry!"

Without arguing the two girls maneuvered the Rebel between them and half-pulling, half-dragging, made their way out the back door, slowly tottering down the path toward the cave. Kirsten quickly emptied the basin and tossed bloody bandages into the fireplace where they shriveled and blackened into pale wisps of nothing.

None too soon she heard a pounding on the front door. With a frantic glance at the rear window, she noticed the staggering figures just disappear into the cave.

Patting her disheveled hair nervously, she hurried to the door. Two Federal soldiers sat erect on their horses while a third stood straight and ramrod tall before her.

"We understand you're harboring a Rebel

soldier, Miss," the captain snapped. "We've come to search the premises. You know it won't bode well for you if we find him."

With a sharp breath Kirsten drew her chin up firmly. "So what if we were? The man stumbled into our barn yesterday. He was badly wounded, and would've died, had we not helped him. But he's not here," she added quickly. "You're welcome to search the house, if you don't believe me.

Without a word, the two men on horseback followed the captain indoors. They slammed doors and checked closets, making rounds of both upstairs and down. Once the captain started for the rear door, and Kirsten's heart almost stopped. Then he turned back.

"We're satisfied no one's here. Sorry we bothered you," he growled, and they stomped out of the house, jumped on their horses, and rode away.

Wearily Kirsten slumped into a chair and placed her head between her hands. *Thank you, dear Lord. . . .* Then she realized the full impact of their act of Christian kindness.

18

It was Friday morning, September 19. When Kirsten came downstairs, her fears of the past week had faded, but she felt drained from the tension. She met a tearful Lieselotte who sat at the table, wringing her hands.

"Lelo — what's wrong? Is it Martin?" Kirsten asked, a new fear surging through her.

"I sat up with him until midnight," Lelo sobbed. "He was sleeping soundly and I thought it was safe to grab some sleep myself. When I awoke he was gone."

"Gone!" Kirsten's hand flew to her throat. "Where is he? Did he say anything — "

"Last night, before he fell asleep, he told me — he told me he loved me. Oh, you heard him. He said he would never forget our kindness, and how we had saved his life. It seems he'd had a sore throat when he came, which made him feel even worse."

Kirsten sat down, propping her elbows on the table and cupping her chin in her hands. That was probably the pneumonia. No wonder he'd been feverish.

"Gone? But we burned his clothes, remember?" she said.

"I checked the closet. Some of Papa's were missing."

"He knew that his being here was dangerous for us, so he left," Kirsten said slowly.

"Yes, but he was still ill. If he could've waited a few more days — "

"He ate quite heartily yesterday. I was amazed at his appetite. After the bullet was gone, he improved rapidly. Perhaps he isn't as ill as we might think," Kirsten said in a reassuring voice. It was amazing that the wound was healing so well, without a sign of infection.

Tears slid down Lelo's rosy cheeks and she paused to wipe them away. "Oh, Kirsten — I knew from the moment I met Martin Druse at Millers that day he was right for me! And now — "

"If he's right for you, he'll come back some day." She got up from the table and went for her bonnet. "After I help Andrew with the chores, I'll scout around the countryside. Maybe I can find out what's happened to

Peter. Andrew said last night there's so much to learn. I hope Papa and David stay away a few more days — at least, until the able-bodied soldiers have all moved out."

"I wonder what made the blue-coats think Martin was here," Lelo wondered aloud.

"Perhaps someone overheard me when I let it slip — that night I went for help."

Somehow she was sure, that, as angry as Wil Patten had been, he was not guilty of turning Martin in to the Union officers.

Heidi had come downstairs during the two girls' conversation, after being persuaded last night that the worst danger was past and she needed to hide in the cave no longer. Now she pattered into the kitchen.

"Could we have sausages and flapjacks?" she asked, and Kirsten noticed the haunting fear had left her eyes.

"I'll let you two fix whatever you wish." With that, she went out to help Andrew tend the animals.

An hour later she saddled Polly and rode around the bend toward the church, apprehension and awe gripping her with every hoofbeat.

There lay the trampled fields; gone were the unmistakable sounds of retreat — the cadence of marching feet, the rumble of caissons where the slow, moving line of butternut and gray had moved down the turnpike.

As she neared the church Kirsten was in time to see a Federal and a Confederate officer shake hands declaring a truce, called to allow both sides to collect their dead and wounded. Already the sun was high in the sky and the heat of the day would soon blaze down.

Seated on her horse on the fringe of the West Woods, Kirsten's disbelieving eyes took in the carnage spread out before her. In front of her the pike was empty, save for the dead and dying. Ambulances rumbled down the road from the battlefields, followed by private carriages commandeered by the medical corps, packed with wounded, and dripping blood in the dust as they jolted over the bumpy road.

Her mouth grew dry at the horrible sight as she rode slowly toward the church. Andrew was right. On the south side, near the roof, several gaping holes made by shot and shell marred the prim exterior. Something compelled her to go inside. With wooden legs she slid from her horse and stepped through the south entrance which she had entered so many times in the past.

The groans of wounded soldiers and cries of the dying rushed to greet her together with the odor of death that permeated the simple house of worship. The table in front was being used for surgery, the large German Bible gone. Draped along the pews were soldiers, some clutching bellies where blood had glued their torn uniforms to gaping wounds. She shrank back, clapping her hand to her mouth, feeling she was going to vomit. Everywhere doctors and male nurses were working feverishly over them. A quick wild glance assured Kirsten that Wilshire Patten was not among them. She shuddered. What an inferno of pain and smell and noise!

Glancing up, Kirsten saw the verse from Psalm 23: *Der Herr Ist Mein Hirte . . . The Lord Is My Shepherd* — and gaping from the exact center of the word *Mein — My —* was a jagged shell hole. Was it an omen? What was God telling her? And horror swept through her again.

She ran back to her horse and rode on. Peter! Where was he? Was he among the blue-coated men who still lay on the ridge along the fences? Whose beards were stiff with blood and from whose broken jaws came ragged screams of "water"?

"Sister Weber!" Someone spoke her name. "What are you doing here?"

She turned to see Thomas Geeting stepping cautiously over dead bodies as he came toward her.

"Brother Geeting!" she cried. "I'm looking for — Peter. I thought maybe — "

"Better go home. This is no place for you — unless you want to be a nurse and help the doctors." He tipped his black wide-brimmed hat. "I was just on my way to check on you and the children. Elder Mumma suggested — "

"We — we're safe — fine. But — it's so horrible. . . . The — the Mummas?"

"They got out safely. I came across the body of a drummer boy on the north side of the church with a bullet hole in his forehead. He wasn't more than 17. His lips were pressed tightly, and his eyes were half open. Still, he wore a bright smile. Beside him lay his drum."

"Peter?" she whispered. "But he wasn't a drum — "

"No." He shook his head. "This was a Rebel. But I've seen the Miller cornfield. That beautiful corn! The biggest part of the field was cut as close as could've been done with a knife, and the dead lay in rows exactly as they had stood in their ranks a few moments before they fell. And so many wounded. . . ."

Undoubtedly soldiers whom Dr. Patten

had treated at the Miller hospital, she thought.

"But the battle at Sunken Road was even worse — if that's possible! That's the road that leads to the old Orndoff Mill, you know, and down which the Rebels stormed to attack the Yankees. But they were doomed from the start when Federal reserves chased them. They say Rebels were piled two and three feet deep, mowed down like grass before a scythe."

Kirsten's mouth dropped open in horror. Death — everywhere, where bodies rotted unburied. . . . And to think God had spared them in their farmhouse behind the hill. *Thank you, God. . . .*

She moistened her dry lips with her tongue. "Is there — anything we can do?"

"With so many wounded — there must be thousands of them — the doctors need so much nursing help. Many of our congregation are helping care for the wounded. And they need food too."

She drew a deep breath. "I'll go home for supplies, then I'll come back and help. Will you let me know if you find out anything about Peter?"

"Of course, Sister Weber."

With that, she turned Polly resolutely toward home.

19

With a bitter taste in her mouth Kirsten rounded the bend and rode into the yard. Lelo rushed out to meet her.

"Any word of Peter?" she cried.

Kirsten shook her head. "We know he was with the ambulance corps. But Brother Geeting has promised to search."

Coming into the house, she hurried to the linen cupboard and drew out several bed sheets. "Here, Lelo. You and Heidi start tearing strips for bandages while I fix a pot of soup. I'm going back to the church to help with nursing and feeding. They need help desperately."

"Our good sheets, Kirsten?" Lelo fumed. "But we have spent hours hem — "

"There are hundreds of wounded men, Lelo," Kirsten snapped. "They *need* bandages! In fact, I saw some soldiers with nothing but *green corn leaves for dressing on raw wounds!* So what if we hem more sheets for ourselves?" Her voice was hoarse with anger.

"Oh, Kirsten — nursing's awful. Do you think you're up to it — after Martin?" Lelo said in a small voice.

"Miss Barton helped nurse in Wil Patten's regiment. I must do it too, Lelo!" she replied firmly.

She got out a panful of potatoes and turnips which she peeled and diced into the pot of beef simmering over the fireplace, and soon the aroma of hearty beef soup drifted through the kitchen. Going to the cave, she came back with several loaves of bread and three jars of raspberry jam. Half an hour later, she had packed the food into the little two-wheeled gig. Turning to her sisters she said, "Keep rolling bandages. And tell Andrew to look after the stock. I'll spend the day at the church doing whatever's necessary."

She pulled on her black bonnet and climbed into the gig, urging Polly down the dusty lane, and praying as she drove. She knew nursing meant groans, delirium, death and smells, and impromptu hospitals filled with dirty, bewhiskered, verminous men who stank horribly and whose bodies bore wounds hideous enough to turn her stomach. But she knew they needed help.

Reaching the church-hospital, she picked up her kettle of soup and carried it to the south entrance. A dirty, unkempt orderly barred her on the threshold.

"Whaddaya think you're doin', lady?" he barked, pushing her back.

"I've come to offer my services as a nurse," she said resolutely. "You need — "

"Nurse? You? Well, the sight ye'll see will make ya sick too," he grumbled. "Besides, we don't need no females — "

"Let her help," one of the doctors muttered from the dim interior. "We need all the help we can get. She can help feed, bathe, or whatever's to be done."

The orderly reluctantly stepped aside, mumbling something about "wimmin takin' over jobs that belong to men" and Kirsten carried in her steaming kettle of soup. She went back to the gig for cups and spoons and the loaves of bread.

"I brought food and bandages," she told the surgeon who seemed to be in charge.

"God bless you, my dear," he said in a harried, brisk way. "I'm Major Dunn, chief surgeon. You're an angel of mercy."

The church swam with the sound of milling feet of doctors and aides, the groans and screams from the men on the operating table. Flies and gnats hovered in droning, singing swarms, tormenting the men with mangled bodies who lay on the pews and who spat out curses and choked on weak sobs.

The tide of smells and pain rose around her as she went about the room, offering cups of soup and slices of bread. Some of the less badly wounded tore the food greedily from her hands while others gagged at the sight of it, their vomit gushing over her clean, freshly starched blue dress.

After she had made the rounds with food, she carried the empty kettle back to the gig and brought in her supply of bandages.

"Here!" ordered Major Dunn, nodding into her direction, "bring me a basin!"

Kirsten dropped the bandages and picked up a pan from a pile of tin utensils in one corner and hurried toward him, hearing screams from the operating area where amputations were going on. She stood beside the doctor, turning her eyes away, trying not to vomit as his scalpel cut into putrid flesh. She felt nausea rise from her stomach and fought to keep from erupting it onto the floor. Perspiration soaked through her dress as the surgeon plunged bloody sponges into the basin and squeezed them dry before daubing the gaping wound where a leg had recently been severed.

She saw amputated arms and legs stacked by the east windows — and the sight in the stuffy room sent her reeling outdoors for fresh air. She leaned against the church's east wall until the lurching of her stomach subsided. With a shake of her head, she surveyed her dress, blood-stained and caked with vomit from the wounded. It had been clean this morning. The sickish, sweet smell of gangrene clung to her hands and hair and she gagged. Why had she promised to help?

Her eyes suddenly moved to the pike and the ridge beyond it. Lying in the pitiless hot sun, shoulder to shoulder, head to feet, were hundreds of wounded men, stretched out in endless rows. Some lay stiff and still, but many writhed and moaned. Everywhere swarms of flies hovered over them, crawling, buzzing in their faces. All Kirsten could see was blood and dirty bandages where first-aid had been performed, and heard groans, curses, and screams of pain as stretcher bearers lifted them into ambulances. The odor of sweat, of blood, of unwashed bodies and excrement rose up on waves of blistering heat until the stench sent her staggering behind the church where she heaved up her breakfast. Leaning her head on her arm, she braced herself against the whitewashed brick walls and drew a long deep breath. *Some nurse you are,* she scolded herself after the nausea had spent itself. *So this is what war is!*

Then she marched back into the church. I won't keel under again, she vowed when the sick, helpless sense of pity at the sight of tense, white faces belonging to mangled bodies confronted her. As they waited for the surgeon the smell of chloroform grew heavy in the operating area and harsh words, "This leg'll have to come off" grated in their ears. The close, stuffy room compounded by tobacco fumes, damp woolen uniforms and unwashed bodies gradually numbed her. She knew chloroform was scarce and used only for the worst amputations, and opium pills were rare. It was now given only to ease dying men out of their life, not the living out of pain.

Kirsten found a clean pail and went out to the well beside the church and drew water. With a dipper, she carried the water from one wounded man to another. Some grabbed the dipper desperately and poured the cooling liquid over their burning, feverish bodies — bodies that were distended, rotten with disease, and almost as repulsive as bleeding wounds that gaped and festered.

Some men crawled with lice, and she was forced to wash bodies with strong lye soap to clear away their misery. Fresh wounded soldiers were brought in, including Rebels, whose faces were black with powder stains, dust and sweat, their wounds unbandaged and accompanied by flies that swarmed everywhere. A few, still able to be on their feet, tottered into the hospital, sank down, croaking "water!"

Before the day was over, Kirsten had learned to bandage stumps and pick maggots out of festering flesh.

When the doctors ran out of bandages, she hopped into the gig and hurried home for the neat rolls Lelo and Heidi had torn from good sheets. She also showed them how to prepare lint to be used as wound dressings. Made from small squares of old linen, then unraveled, lint was placed directly into wounds to prevent them from healing because it was thought healing could take place only after formation of "laudable pus."

"Your dress looks absolutely filthy," Heidi accused as Kirsten stood beside them, pulling at threads in squares of old linen. "You must be working awfully hard."

Kirsten shook her head. "It's so terrible, you wouldn't believe it. Clara Barton was right. But someone must do it. I'll change into a clean dress before I go back."

Two days passed. Each morning Kirsten prepared more food, more bandages, and set out to help. On the third day when she walked into the hospital with another supply of bandages and lint she saw a kind, elderly man go from one wounded soldier to the next, and speak to each one.

"Who is he, and what's he doing?" Kirsten asked one of the orderlies who had come to welcome her help.

"Him? That's Chaplain George Bullen. It's his job to care for the men's souls, like it's ours to look after their bodies."

At least the men will learn about God's love, she thought.

He opened his Bible, read a few Scriptures, and bowed his head to pray. Now and then she heard joyful shouts; but sometimes curses from cracked, swollen lips sent him, grim-faced, to the next soldier.

As Kirsten bent down and washed dried blood and caked dirt from grimy faces, she slowly grew accustomed to the stench, the verminous bodies and the hands that clutched swollen stomachs with matted blood stuck to uniforms. She held wobbling hands and poured water over dusty, feverish faces. She even dribbled whiskey between swollen lips to dull their pain. The air was stagnant, and dust clogged her nostrils from ambulances that rumbled up the pike with a new load of wounded and dying and dislodged their gruesome burdens, gnats and mosquitoes swarming over each bloody face. Every time she looked up anxiously for a glimpse of Peter; each time she was disappointed.

One soldier lay with his pocket Bible on his chest, turned to Psalm 23. She picked it up and read the underlined words: " 'Yea, though I walk through the valley of the shadow of death, I will fear no evil: for thou art with me; thy rod and thy staff they comfort me.' " On the flyleaf were the words: *We hope and pray that you may be permitted by kind Providence after the war is over, to return.* Tears ran down her tired cheeks as she saw the glazed look in the soldier's eyes, the chest unmoving, and she gently pressed the eyelids down.

Completing his rounds, Chaplain Bullen drew off his blue cap, wiped the sweat from his brow, and bowed politely to Kirsten.

"I've admired your quiet nursing, your courageous care of these wounded," he said. "Surely, you must remind the men of some sweetheart or wife or sister left behind!"

Kirsten managed a wan smile and drew

off her bonnet. "You should've seen me two days ago. There was nothing brave about me then!"

"Tell me, who are you, and why are you doing this — a beautiful young member of the Baptist Brethren, who certainly doesn't believe in war."

"My name's Kirsten Weber. Why am I doing this? Christ said, 'Inasmuch as ye have done it unto one of the least of these my brethren, ye have done it unto me.' My brother Peter left us to join General McClellan's Army of the Potomac in the ambulance corps. Perhaps I'm a bit selfish, but I'm hoping to catch sight of Peter somewhere."

"Peter? Weber?" A puzzled frown crept across the chaplain's lined forehead. "God be praised. I met a young man by that name who was wounded while carrying a dying man toward his ambulance when a bullet struck him in the back. As I talked to him, he said, 'Tell my family — I'm happy doing what I wanted to do — and that I love them very much.' Then he died."

"Died!" Kirsten whispered hoarsely. "Peter — dead!" She sank to her knees and buried her face in her hands and wept.

Chaplain Bullen laid a gentle hand on her shoulder. "I'm so sorry. It happened as

General Burnside was attempting to cross the bridge over the Antietam. But if you'd seen the look of radiance on his face — "

"Peter — dead," Kirsten repeated dully, feeling numb. Then she raised her eyes. "Where is his body? Do you know — where he's buried?"

"I personally saw to it that he was buried, and spoke a few words from the Scriptures over his grave and prayed. Some day I'll show you his resting place."

She knew that vast acres of farmland would become massive cemeteries before the war was over.

As the hot day wore on, Kirsten's back ached and her knees buckled with weariness. The curls had crept from her bun and hung damply in her face. And now that the grim words beat into her spirit she broke down and wept some more. Why hadn't she kept Peter from leaving? Not only had she lost Captain Wilshire Patten; her own brother lay buried on the rocky hillside near the bridge over the Antietam.

As she drove her gig home that night, she felt lower than at any time since the battle had begun. How could she face her family with the horrible news of Peter's death?

After she stabled Polly and started for the house, she heard the rumble of the farm wagon and the team's familiar neighing. Papa! David Poffenberger had brought her father home at last. Dear God, Kirsten cried, how can I tell Papa that Peter is dead?

She ran to the wagon and hugged him tightly, then stood back to look at him. He looked gaunt and haggard. Between her and David they helped him into the house and laid him on his bed. Kirsten noticed David's gentleness, his tender lifting and care of her father, and for that she was grateful.

One thing she knew. She would stay home and nurse Papa. With his aggravated case of dysentery he needed special nursing care. She would put off telling him about Peter as long as she could. Tomorrow. I'll tell him tomorrow, she decided. Yet she need not have worried. He was so exhausted he promptly fell asleep.

20

A cold gray sky greeted Kirsten when she awoke one morning in early November, shivering under the warm comforts. The morning came dim and late, and as she walked down the stairs the huge grate of the fireplace was black with burned-out logs. She quietly built a brisk fire that soon snapped and crackled merrily.

Hearing Papa stirring in his bedroom she hurried in to see what he wanted. His eyes looked drawn and hollow, for the dysentery had become chronic.

"How are you this morning, Papa?" she said cheerfully as she entered his room. He was sitting on the edge of the bed, his blankets skewered into a pile around his knees.

"I've been home seven weeks, and still no better," he said with a weary sigh. "When I think how foolish I was to leave you to manage the farm while I did what I felt was

God's work, I shudder. Had I been home, I might have kept Peter from leaving." His voice was ragged and bitter.

"No, Papa." Kirsten picked a warm flannel shirt from the nail in his closet and drew the sleeves over his thin, bare arms, "Peter was determined to leave, and no one could have done anything to stop him. He did what he had to do. I'm sure he didn't think it would lead to — death." It had been hard to tell her father that Peter had slipped out one night while he was gone to join the ambulance corps, and of his subsequent death. The family had mourned for days, knowing the young, slightly built boy would never be home again.

"Death. . . ." Papa echoed. "Oh, Kirsten, I'd counted on him to carry on the work of the farm some day. Now — "

"Now you can count on Andrew. He's been remarkable, Papa. I couldn't have managed without him." She helped Papa into his trousers and led him into the dining room to his rocking chair by the fire. Ever since his return, he had spent all his time in bed or in his rocker. Yet the farm was always uppermost in his mind.

"Well, you're very dependable, Kirsten, but Andrew is too young for heavy work. Besides, he must finish school, once it opens again."

He leaned back in his chair, his eyes closed, face white as parchment. Kirsten thought, *Will Papa succumb to this illness? What will happen to us if he leaves us too?* She went to the kitchen and began breakfast preparations.

"I've been thinking," he said suddenly. "If you marry David Poffenberger, he could take over the farm. The house is large and there's plenty of room here for you and us both."

A cold hand swept over Kirsten's spine at his words. David had asked her to marry him more than once, and for all practical purposes it was the best solution. Yet why did she resist the thought of marrying this kind, gentle Christian? Of course, she'd continue to look after the family just as she had since their mother's death. As usual, Papa couldn't do without her help. There were no bride dreams for a home of her own — with the man she loved . . . *the man she loved* — who no longer loved her . . . whom she might never see again. . . .

"Kirsten?" Papa called. "Did you hear what I just said?"

"Yes, Papa." Kirsten paused with slicing ham for frying.

"It would be the perfect solution. You would have my most profound blessing.

David is a fine young man, for I learned to know him well during the time he nursed me on the long way back from Washington. Don't you think?"

Kirsten's words stuck in her throat. "I — yes, it would solve many — problems. But — but — "

"He loves you devotedly. Nothing would please me more."

"I — Papa, I had always planned — to be married in the church. It — it won't be in shape for a long time."

"Well, there are other churches, like the Manor Church. Don't let a mere building stop you."

She placed the thin slices of ham in the iron skillet and pushed it over the front burner of the range. What of it? David was all Papa said he was — and more. He would be a good husband, one who worked hard to provide for her needs. And he loved her. *Then why am I hesitating?* She asked herself.

Swallowing hard, she came into the dining room and stood before her father, hands on her hips, her lips drawn into a thin line.

"Let me think about it, Papa. Marriage is a grave step, something I must be sure is right. Please don't rush me."

Dear Lord, she prayed, *show me what to do. Is this your will? Or do you have another an-*

swer? But first things first.

Papa needed help desperately, for he was so ill. He seemed to be growing worse slowly. And he would want his answer soon.

The next morning she decided to go to Sharpsburg for Dr. Biggs. It was the first time she had gone into town since before the battle, and it proved to be a devastating experience. Andrew had ridden in weekly for the mail and other supplies.

She saw the naked shell holes in the buildings and shops, for many of the houses were hit by shot and shell of Union cannon. She counted eleven shell holes in the Antietam Hotel which General Lee had used as a Council of War headquarters, and saw where a shot had been fired into Aaron Fry's home. It had come through the building, passed through a door, and into a chest of bedlinens. When a bed sheet was unfolded later there was a shell hole in every fold of the sheet, they said.

With a shudder she hurried across the street to Dr. Bigg's stone house. The sign: *Dr. A. A. Biggs,* hung crookedly above the battered door. She could see the large hole torn through the wall even before she reached it.

"Doctor's not here," Edward Reilly told her, picking up debris that lay scattered everywhere. "He's helping dress wounded in the field hospitals. Help's been so scarce. I don't know when he'll be back." Then he went on to tell her what had happened the day of the battle.

"We was on top of Elk Ridge, the Union Signal Station. Here we had a good view of the whole battlefield. We seen great columns of smoke and dust as the armies surged forward, and was pushed back. The next day me and my boy walked over the field, and we seen where soldiers had crawled into bushes and died there. Some was buried so shallow that their heads stuck out. Then I guess you heard about the awful things that happened at John Kretzers'."

"No." Kirsten shook her head. She wasn't sure she wanted to hear more.

Ignoring her disinterest, Reilly went on. "Miz Henry Ward had just given birth to a baby shortly before the shootin' started. People crowded into the Kretzer basement to escape. I guess at least two hundred folks was crammed down there. Then some of the women decided it was too damp for Miz Ward in her delicate condition and took her back upstairs. She was there only a few minutes when a shell tore through the kitchen, nearly blinding her with dust and smoke. She screamed so loud that John Kretzer rushed up to see what had happened. She said she'd rather be downstairs where it was damp, and take a chance on taking cold and dyin' than be killed by cannon fire!"

Kirsten turned away and shut her ears to the awful atrocities that had happened that day. And there had been many. Again she was grateful to God that he had kept them safe behind the hill.

Nauseated, she turned away and hurried home. I'll never be the same again, she told herself. Furthermore, the statistics staggered her imagination. Nearly 23,000 soldiers were killed or wounded in that one-day battle on September 17.

Kirsten had learned some other startling facts that both alarmed and amazed her. Although both North and South fought furiously, neither dared claim total victory. General McClellan's overcautiousness had robbed the Yankees of the prize that could have brought the war to a speedier close, for Federals far outnumbered Confederates. Yankee soldiers were better trained and equipped. Why Little Mac hadn't taken advantage of his army's superiority was hard to understand.

President Lincoln's patience with General McClellan's lack of initiative was exhausted. On November 5 he had removed the general from command and appointed Ambrose Burnside as his successor, for Burnside seemed more willing to accept challenges.

"If Ol'Burnside had been in charge in the first place instead of Little Mac," Elias Smith maintained when his customers traded at his general store, "the Antietam Battle might not have been so fiercely bloody."

Yes, there was no doubt about it. The Battle of Antietam had changed all their lives. Worst of all, Kirsten's errand to find a much-needed doctor for her father had been in vain.

The days wore on, and between nursing Papa and supervising the work on the place, she had little time to think.

She sensed that Papa was slowly growing worse in spite of all she could do for him. Was there no remedy, no help for his condition?

Allie Mumma's surprise visit later that afternoon lifted her lagging spirits.

"Allie!" She embraced her friend warmly. "What's happened to you since that awful day last September?"

"So many things I'll never be able to tell them all — funny things too!" she lilted.

Trust Allie to see the bright side, Kirsten thought as the two girls sat down before the fire. Papa was in bed most of the time now, and Lelo was in a corner, reading a book as usual. Andrew was outdoors and Heidi laboriously knitted a pair of red socks by the south window.

"Lizzie was with us that awful day, and when the Rebels came, they vowed to burn our farm — can you imagine it? — to keep Union sharpshooters from using the buildings. Lizzie and I grabbed a few trinkets and hurried out the back door. When we ran toward the fence, a Rebel soldier popped up and wanted to be gallant and help us over, but we told him, 'No, thanks — we don't need you!' and we scrambled over without any help. Maybe we weren't very ladylike, but we were angry, being driven from our home so they could burn it down."

"Yes, I saw the flames from the hill that day," Kirsten said. "I was worried about you."

"We escaped to the Hoffman farm and later to the Manor Church. Since then we've lived on the Sherrick farm because the Sherricks have pulled out for good. But we did help the Hoffman ladies bake cakes and pies, and brought food and fruit to the wounded who lay in their barn."

"I assumed you were all right, Allie. But with Papa's illness I've been tied down."

"*Ach,* I know. That's why I came out today. Did you hear about the time General Hood sent a soldier up a tree in the East Woods to determine how big the Union Army was? The man looked down and said, 'There are oceans of them!' Whereupon Stonewall Jackson muttered, 'Never mind the oceans. Just count the battle flags.' He began to count flags and when he got to 37, Jackson snorted, 'That will do! Come on down and we'll get out of here quick!' When I heard that, I laughed so hard my side hurt for a week!"

Trust Allie to see humor in even the most devastating circumstances. Then Allie's face sobered. "I hear you helped nurse the wounded hospitalized in our church. That must've been quite a strain."

"It was awful. Not only were they Union wounded — we also took care of some Rebels after my first day. But I helped only until David brought Papa home. Since then I've tried to nurse my father."

"How is he?"

"Not well at all. He needs a good doctor, but the few doctors here are so very busy, taking care of injured soldiers."

"Any word of your Doctor Patten, Kirsten?" Allie asked bluntly.

Kirsten bit her underlip sharply before

answering. "He isn't *my* Captain Patten, Allie!" she flared. "I found out he was in the field hospital on the Daniel Miller farm and when Andrew and I braved the danger to ask him to help Martin Druse, he almost threw me out. Oh, Allie — I've been so miserable!"

"What's the next step? What do you plan to do about it?"

With a shake of her bright head, Kirsten lowered her gaze. "I honestly don't know. Papa wants me to marry David Poffenberger. We need someone to do the heavy work, and it would be the perfect solution."

"And what do *you* think?"

"Oh, Allie, I'm so confused. I know it would solve our problems but — " she paused.

"But what, Kirsten?"

"I don't love David. Somehow I dread to think of being married to a man I don't love. Especially — "

"Especially since you still love Doctor Patten? Is that it?"

"I — I suppose you're right. I'm praying for the solution, Allie,"

"It will come, Kirsten. God never comes too late."

Somehow after Allie left, Kirsten felt encouraged. Whatever the Lord's answer, it would be the right one.

21

One brisk afternoon a week later, David Poffenberger came over. Kirsten let him into the warm house and took his wraps. With a gentle smile he held her hands in his own, then followed her into the parlor. He stood before her, declining the proffered chair.

"Wait, Kirsten. I've meant to come for weeks but there's been so much to do, helping clean up the aftermath. Some things will never be the same again."

"I know. What about the church? Is it worth repairing?"

"Oh, yes, but it will take time. There are hospitals everywhere. It seems every home or church housed the wounded. Even the Pry farm was used as a hospital, although the more badly injured have been moved to the hospital at Frederick, you know. Since Dr. Jonathan Letterman has been made medical director of the army, he has initiated many changes, most of them good."

"Didn't McClellan have his headquarters at Philip Pry's?"

"Yes. The place sits astride a hill which gave him an excellent view of the valley where the terrible fighting went on. But as I said, there's been so much debris to clear away, and so many dead to be buried that it will take months to bring a semblance of order to Washington County again. In spite of all this, I couldn't stay away any longer, Kirsten. How is your father?"

Kirsten shook her head. "Not good, David. I feel he's failing gradually. Besides, he's worried about — about the farm, with Peter gone."

"Kirsten. . . ." David began slowly, nervously. "Kirsten, why don't you marry me? I could move in here with you and tackle the big jobs on the farm. I'm sure your father would approve."

A deep sigh shook her and she moistened her dry lips. "It would — obviously be the perfect solution. But — but I must be sure it's God's will. I — I can't pretend to love you when I don't, David. To me, marriage must be based on more than mutual respect."

"I see." He laced his fingers together and stared unseeing at the floor. "I've proposed marriage before and you've always put me off. Kirsten — " he looked up suddenly and placed his hands on her shoulders. "Kirsten, is there — someone else?"

"S-someone else?" she stammered, her face flooding with red color. "Oh, David — you're the dearest, the gentlest of all men, and I don't understand why I cannot fall in love with you. But. . . ." How can I go on, and tell him that my heart belongs to Wilshire Patten? she agonized silently.

"But — what, Kirsten? There *is* someone, isn't there? Who is he? Can you tell me, my dear?"

Kirsten shook her head helplessly. How could she admit to something she barely understood herself? She ran her tongue over her dry lips.

"David — over a year ago when Polly threw me and I injured my ankle, it was Dr. Wilshire Patten who happened along and treated it. He brought me home, and he — we fell in love. I — it was something I resisted and told myself it was just a foolish whim. Yet I knew it was love of the purest kind. Wil says he loves me but does not share my faith in Christ. As long as he doesn't, I cannot marry him. Besides, his social standing is far above mine. But — all I know is that — that I love him, and no one else could ever take his place in my heart." *Even though he may have stopped loving me now*, she reminded herself.

David dropped his hands slowly. "I — see. So — that's the way it is." His voice sounded dead.

"Oh, David, I'm so sorry! I only wish it were different," she cried.

"So do I. But as long as I know you care for him, I could never be truly happy, knowing you'd pretend it was Patten who was holding you when you were in my arms. . . ." His voice broke.

Kirsten turned away, unable to watch the anguish in his face. *Dear God, why did it have to be so hard? Why didn't you make me love David instead of Wil?*

David started for the door. "But if you change your mind, Kirsten. . . . I'll pray for God to show you what to do. Meanwhile — " He turned to look at her once more, a deep pained yearning light in his eyes, then walked toward the front door and left.

Without a word Kirsten watched him go, staring at his departing figure for a long minute.

Lelo glanced up from her book. "What was that all about, Kirsten? He looked as though he's lost his best friend."

"Maybe he has," Kirsten said quietly.

"Maybe he has," she said again as she started for the stairs.

"Kirsten?" Papa's voice called weakly from the bedroom.

With a smothered sigh she turned around and went to her father's room. "Yes, Papa?"

"Wasn't that David Poffenberger's voice I heard? I thought perhaps he would stop to see me."

Kirsten turned her face away. "He — asked about you," she said in a low voice. Then, summoning her courage for what she knew she must say, she went on. "Papa, David asked me to marry him. I told him I couldn't."

"Couldn't!" Papa's voice creaked with weakness. "Or wouldn't? If it's because the church won't be ready for a good while — "

"No, it's not that. It's — it's because I don't love David Poffenberger. That's why, Papa."

"But — but surely you can learn to love — "

"God only knows, I've fought it, and have tried to deny it to myself over and over, but it doesn't do any good. Papa, I'm afraid I love Dr. Wilshire Patten, and always shall."

"Dr. Patten!" Papa cried, jerking himself to a sitting position. "But he — he's an unbeliever, a man totally different from German Baptists! We were in his home, you

235

know. His family are good people, but he'd never fit into our lifestyle, Kirsten — even if he did believe. Don't you see that?"

"Does it mean he'd have to adjust to *our* lifestyle? Couldn't I adjust to his?" she demanded, astonished at her own brash words.

Weakly Papa fell back onto the bed. "My child, this is — a terrible blow. I'd counted on David's taking over the farm. . . ."

"But you never figured on my not agreeing with your plans," she cut in harshly. "Oh, Papa — Papa, I didn't ever want to hurt you, but don't you see? If I married David while loving another man, I'd commit a grave sin — both against David and against God. The Lord wants us to follow his leading. That's exactly what I plan to do."

She moved to the bed, stooped over, and gently kissed his pale forehead. Then she turned and walked slowly from the room. She knew she'd hurt her father too. Could she really fit into Wil's lifestyle? She honestly didn't know. But of course, perhaps Wil had stopped caring.

The next move is yours, Lord, she agonized. *I'm waiting for you to show me. If it's David, then so be it.* Again she started for the stairs.

At a sharp rap on the front door, she paused. Who was it this time?

236

When she opened it, a familiar jaunty figure stood on the threshold, a merry smile on his face.

"Martin Druse! What are you doing here?" she cried, reaching out her hand. "Do come in."

Lelo jumped up from her chair and flew to the door. "Martin — it's really you, isn't it?"

"I'm no ghost, Lelo," he said, stepping indoors. He doffed his ragged gray army cap and the auburn curls tumbled across his forehead. "I just had to come to thank you for the fine care you gave me — was it only two months ago? You see, I'm fine and I've regained my strength completely. But an injured nerve leading to my right arm will keep me from ever carrying a gun again."

Kirsten pulled out a chair and motioned him toward it. "Sit down and tell us what's happened since you sneaked out of here that miserable Friday morning."

A boyish grin lit up his face again. "I did sneak out, didn't I? And Lelo never even noticed! Well, when I realized I was jeopardizing your integrity and position, and perhaps your safety, I had to leave before I got you into a deeper mess. So I began walking. I was pretty tired that first day because my wound was still raw and sore, but the awful pain was gone. I watched my chances and crept through enemy lines. Tottering along and wearing your father's old clothes made me look like a drunken old farmer — and no one bothered me."

"Martin — you didn't!" Lelo chided. "But weren't you almost dead by the time you reached home? I worried so!"

"Oh, I was tired, all right, but my mother's a good nurse. In fact, she nursed several other wounded people who happened along our farm. One was a Union army surgeon, a Dr. Patten. He — "

"Wil Patten!" Kirsten cried. She felt the color drain from her cheeks, "He was — hurt?"

"A stray bullet struck his left hand. He was a very nice chap, and so polite, but quite discouraged." Martin grew quiet. Then with another quick grin, he said, "I wondered if you folks need a good farmhand. I heard about your brother Peter, and since I know all about farming, I thought maybe I could — sort of — "

Kirsten's heart began to hammer furiously, This was God's doing! If Martin managed the heavy work, that problem would be solved. It meant she needn't feel guilty about not marrying David. But to think the Druse family had compassion enough to care for a wounded Union Army surgeon was what really mattered.

With a quick gesture, Kirsten clasped Martin's strong hand in hers. "You're just what we've been looking for, Martin Druse — an answer to our prayers. How soon can you start?"

"As soon as I get my things."

He took Kirsten's hand and gave it a firm squeeze, then picked up Lelo's two hands and held them gently for a long while. Replacing his cap, he whirled around and swung jauntily out of the house. Lelo stared after him, her heart in her eyes.

Kirsten looked after his retreating figure. It was incredible. What had Allie said last week? The Lord never came too late.

With a buoyant step, Kirsten called to Andrew to begin the evening chores. "I'll come as soon as I can," she added.

Just then she heard pounding hoofbeats on the hard turf of the lane. The familiar black stallion that galloped between the fence rows was unmistakable. For the rider was none other than Doctor Wilshire Patten.

22

Kirsten stood rooted to the ground, unable to move. She had been sure he would never want to see her again, after his cruel words that night on the Miller farm.

He rode slowly now, his horse trotting with an easy canter. The gray afternoon was growing late, and the lowering sun glimmered through thin clouds in the west. The wooded valley to the south lay in dark shadows.

Drawing Beecher up beside her, Wil stopped. His face looked gaunt and thin under the snappy brimmed blue cap and he brushed it back with a weak flourish. The rich brown waves fell across his brow that puckered into its usual questioning look, and Kirsten's heart quickened with love and compassion.

"Kirsten — I came to apologize," he said, sliding from the saddle.

She took his arm gently and led him up the brick paved walk to the front door. "Let's go inside," she said thickly. *I'll cry if I'm not careful,* she told herself.

He followed her meekly into the house, and then she saw he held his left hand inside the half-buttoned opening of his blue uniform.

"Here, have a chair while I tell Lelo to help Andrew with the chores." She noticed he did not sit down, but waited until she came back. Again she motioned to a chair.

"Wait, Kirsten — let me have my say first," he said, standing awkwardly, his voice tired and ragged. "Please forgive me for the harsh way I spoke to you the night you came to the field hospital."

"There's no need — " she began.

"Yes, I know I was rude and thoughtless. But there were so many wounded, and so little we could do for many of them. You hadn't responded to my letters, and I guess I was hurt and angry. Then you asked for my help to dig a bullet out of a *Rebel soldier.* It was too much!" His voice cracked.

"Oh, Wil! I'm sorry. It was I who was thoughtless. I should've realized. . . ."

"No, you had every right to come to me — a doctor. But to know you were there — finally you had come to me, after I hadn't heard a word in months — and I couldn't come near you . . . because there were hundreds of wounded soldiers who needed me worse than you did. I said the first thing that came to mind."

"Please, Wil — I do understand. But I was so desperate — "

"Yes, I know, and the way I treated you was most shameful." He drew out his left arm. A white bandage neatly covered it — until Kirsten saw that *there was no hand,* and a surge of pity swept through her.

"Oh — Wil!" she cried. "I'm so sorry! Martin said you'd wandered to their place where his mother nursed you back to health. But I didn't know — "

"Health!" he said bitterly. "Yes, I've recovered from my — injury, but I can never be a doctor again. All the years of training, of plans for the future — gone! Wiped out by one minié ball!"

She took his right arm and led him to a chair by the window and sat down beside him. "But your mother was so proud of you. She told me — "

"Mother's prejudiced. She has her work cut out helping my stepfather run the factory. But I — " His voice was bitter.

"Please tell me about it," she said gently.

He swallowed hard, and she saw his jaw

muscles working before he spoke. "It must've been about midnight on the 17th of September. Most of the fighting was over, although we heard a few random shots now and then. I went out to the Miller barn filled with wounded who lay moaning on the straw. The doors were open to the stifling heat. As I stooped over to examine one of the injured men, a stray shot suddenly struck my hand out of nowhere. With a cry of pain I stumbled back to the house where the other surgeons were still amputating and operating. Blood gushed from the wound and onto my uniform as I pressed my arm tightly against me. In the dim lantern light I saw that a minié ball had ripped through the center of the palm, severing arteries and cruelly lacerating the flesh."

"Oh, how awful!" Kirsten cried, tears cutting shiny paths down her cheeks.

"I slumped over in a faint, and when I awoke — my hand was gone. One of the surgeons had severed it, just as I had amputated so many limbs that day. . . ." His voice choked. Kirsten watched as the horror of the event crept over his face and she lowered her eyes because she couldn't bear to see his agony.

"What did you do then?" she prodded gently.

"In a daze I staggered to my feet and began to walk. Through the long night I stumbled down roads that seemed to stretch endlessly before me. I had no idea where I was going. Something compelled me to walk on and on. The dark, violent night grew even darker. The opium pill I'd been given for pain had begun to wear off and I felt the horrible throbbing of severed flesh and nerves where my hand had been. Loss of blood and weariness began to overtake me. All I wanted was to lie down and die. Ahead in the pale moonlight I made out the dim outline of a barn. My footsteps quickened as I headed toward this place of refuge. Or maybe I was more like an animal that knows it is dying and looks for a comfortable place to curl up and fall into everlasting oblivion."

He paused, his face taut and gray with the memory. With a shake of his head, he went on. "When I awoke I was lying in bed, and a plump, sweet-faced middle-aged woman was bending over me. I turned my face away, for I wanted only to die. Yet I was afraid of death. How can I ever practice medicine again with only one hand? But — " he sighed deeply.

"But what, Wil?"

"Carrie Druse — I learned the name was Druse — refused to let me die. She nursed me faithfully and tenderly. Yet what I noticed more than anything was God's love in that household. It was almost — tangible, and I couldn't understand it. What struck me most was that I soon became aware that these were — *Confederate sympathizers!* Oh, they knew I was a Yankee; yet that didn't seem to matter. The woman prayed and quoted Scripture. Her favorite passage was the twenty-third Psalm. If I heard it once, I heard it a hundred times: 'Yea, though I walk through the valley of the shadow of death, I will fear no evil: for thou art with me.' I can't understand it, Kirsten. I was the enemy; yet I was treated as though I — mattered!"

Kirsten nodded, tears stinging her eyes. "Yes. That's what God's love does. Galatians 3:28 says, 'There is neither Jew nor Greek, there is neither bond nor free . . . for ye are all one in Christ Jesus' — and to paraphrase it, we'd probably say, 'In Christ there is no North or South' for all who believe in him are one in Christ."

A strange light began to touch his face, and his eyes grew animated and alive. "That's exactly it! I saw God's love demonstrated so clearly in the Druse family, toward me and to the other soldiers Carrie Druse nursed so graciously. I noticed they were not of your faith. And maybe that's how it was with you when you took care of Martin Druse. . . . Still, if that's what Christianity is all about — "

"That's the very essence of it," Kirsten said, her voice thick with tears. "Don't you see, Wil? Faith isn't something that's lived out only in the church, with a bunch of traditions and rules. It's a personal matter, an attitude of the heart. No, the Druses aren't German Baptist Brethren, but they're God's people too. Why wouldn't they show love?"

"I think I'm beginning to understand, Kirsten. God can touch a person with his love even in a vicious war. A war that cost me my hand . . . which does not alter the fact that my work as a doctor is over. All those years of study, the practice of surgery, the many people I've helped — it's hard to believe it's finished."

Kirsten jumped up and placed a hand on Wil's shoulder. "Oh, but it isn't, Wilshire Patten! You may not be able to operate, yet the field of medicine is wide. You can still function — and very capably — as a diagnostician, a medical adviser, or perhaps as a general practitioner. Wil, please believe me — *your life is not over!*"

His face took on the gray hue again, and

Kirsten saw the hopelessness written in the deep lines. "No, Kirsten. Without performing surgery, I'll never be of use to anyone again." With that, he got slowly to his feet, and his tired face broke into a wan smile. "I had once hoped to make you my wife someday, my darling, but when I thought you didn't care — and now I can offer you only half a life . . . I — I know you'll find someone else — yes, I've heard — like David Poffenberger, who can make you happy." He started toward the door.

Kirsten's heart constricted with the pain of never seeing him again. How could she let him go this way? And yet — for both their sakes it was best.

Just then, at a sound from Papa's bedroom, she turned. Papa staggered into the dining room, holding on to chairs and tables as he wobbled along.

"Kirsten" — he croaked weakly. "Kirsten. . . ."

23

With a sudden jerk, Wil whirled on Kirsten and grabbed her left shoulder with his right hand. "What's wrong with your father? He's obviously a very sick man!"

"He came home from Washington in late September with a bad case of dysentery and it's steadily grown worse. I'm afraid my father's dying," she said in a low voice.

"No!" Wil cried, "we can't let him die. In my saddle bag there's a kit of drugs. Bring it in quickly." Even as he spoke, Wil had taken Papa's hand and led him back toward the bedroom.

Praying with each anxious step, Kirsten hurried out for the medical kit. As she came back breathlessly, Papa was on his bed. Wil was taking Papa's pulse, then gently pressed the swollen abdomen with his hand over the clean muslin nightshirt.

Silently he opened his kit and drew out a

vial. Without a word, Kirsten went to the kitchen for a cup of cold water and handed it to the young doctor. After he had completed his examination he helped Albert Weber to a sitting position with his left arm and poured some of the medicine into the cup of water with his right hand.

"Here. Drink this, sir," he said quietly.

After Papa had drained the cup, Wil lifted his eyes toward Kirsten. "Do you have blackberry wine? Or is wine against your tradition? Blackberry root would do as well," he added with obvious embarrassment.

"We have a jug of blackberry wine in the cave," she said distinctly. "I'll send Heidi after it."

He fumbled in his pocket and drew out a piece of paper and pencil, then jotted down a few words and handed it to her. "Follow this diet for your father, Kirsten, plus all the fruit juices he can handle — especially apple juice. It should help him recuperate faster." Then he poured some powder into a small bottle. "And give him a dose of this medication every morning. It's something new which I have tried on my patients and found quite beneficial. Oh — the blackberry wine will help too. It's very therapeutic."

Papa reached out a shaky hand. "Thank God — you came, Dr. Patten," he whispered hoarsely. "I couldn't — leave my — family quite yet, even though Kirsten is very — dependable."

Dependable. There was that word again. Was that all she would ever mean to her family?

"I'll stop by next week to check on you. As your daughter knows — " Will smiled at Kirsten, "I'm a doctor who believes in checking on my patients!"

With that, he picked up his kit and started for the door. Kirsten was at his heels, her gray eyes shining.

"Wil!" she cried, "do you realize what you just did? You've proved that your life as a doctor isn't over!"

"Yes," he said and a crooked grin broke across his gaunt face. "I guess I did. My mother would've been pleased — By the way," he added, and the old whimsical look returned, "you did a magnificent job in removing the minié ball Martin Druse caught in his chest, and the care you gave him was excellent."

Together they walked out to the stallion which stood quietly switching its glossy black tail at the hitching post. He climbed into the saddle and fastened a gentle gaze on Kirsten's face for a moment.

A watercolor sunset had brightened the

soft twilight sky with vivid streaks of orange, pink, and crimson, and long shadows stretched away from the lowering sun.

Kirsten looked up at him. "You'll be back?" she asked anxiously.

"I'll be back — to check on my patient." And with a word to his horse, he wheeled and rode down the lane.

24

The next several days passed by quickly. Kirsten faithfully monitored her father's medication and diet, and to her joy, he slowly grew stronger. Now and then he joined the family at the table.

"If only Peter were here," he sighed one morning after breakfast. "It would be almost like old times."

"Doesn't Martin count?" Lelo asked, her eyes dancing at her mention of the jaunty young farmhand who had arrived to look after the farm work.

"He's a remarkable young man, even if he's a Rebel," Papa conceded, "a tireless worker too. As for work, he easily runs circles around Peter. And he's a devoted Christian — even if he isn't from our church. I must admit he does count."

Martin's coming had relieved Kirsten of her outdoor chores and miraculously Lelo had volunteered to take over some of the cooking. Martin and Andrew worked well together, but Kirsten could scarcely contain her mirth at the way Andrew sometimes bossed the new hand. One afternoon she overheard the twosome as they were grinding axes before going to the woods to chop kindling, for the woodpile had dwindled drastically.

"We don't cut down walnut trees for firewood," Andrew advised nonchalantly, "so stick with cottonwoods and sycamores."

"What's wrong with walnut trees?" Martin asked, his naiveté apparent. "Look, my farm experience don't include much about trees."

"Oh, I wouldn't dream of disturbing the squirrel nests. It makes about as much sense as Rebels roosting along Sunken Lane!"

"Or Burnside trying for *three hours* to cross one measly bridge," Martin shot back.

But their joshing was good-natured, although the fact that the young hand had been a Rebel soldier was something Andrew couldn't forget as easily as Lelo.

Now it was a week before Thanksgiving, but the weather had suddenly turned mild. Each day Kirsten looked toward the bend for the black stallion and its rider, but over a week had gone by.

When Wil Patten rode up bareheaded and tethered Beecher to the hitching post, Kirsten hurried out to meet him.

"Doctor Patten!" she scolded mildly, "I was beginning to think Papa would be well before you got here."

He picked up his medical kit and followed her into the house. "Your father is better, I take it?"

"He's improved remarkably. Of course, he's had a good doctor!" Her gray eyes sparkled.

"And a fine nurse, don't forget. What's he been up to?"

"He takes some meals at the table, and has been out for short walks outdoors, but I make him promise to be back in ten minutes. I think he's had to satisfy himself that Martin Druse is doing his job."

"Good." Wil stopped and placed a hand on her shoulder. "Please tell me what you did to make that Rebel scamp's wound heal so fast. I couldn't believe my eyes how quickly he was well, when he came back home."

"Well, there was no suppuration — "

"You mean — 'first intention'? But most wounds go through a stage of laudable pus. I can't understand why his didn't. How did you remove that bullet?"

Kirsten let out a deep sigh. "It was after Miss Barton gave me that knife and forceps and told me what to do."

"Clara Barton did a noble job, helping us during that terrible day. So that's what happened to the missing instruments!"

"If it hadn't been for her — and for God's grace, I could never have done it," Kirsten added. "I simply washed my hands and the instruments in hot soapy water — "

"Why did you do that?"

"Let me tell you, Dr. Wilshire Patten," she flared, "I'm a scrupulous housekeeper and believe in getting rid of foreign matter with hot water and soap!"

"And I suppose there was foreign matter on the instruments?"

"Why — why, I'd carried them in the pocket of my apron through enemy lines — and couldn't risk contamination," she said a trifle haughtily.

He stared at her, an incredible light in his blue eyes. "H'mmm. I — see! We've scrubbed floors and bedpans and latrines and sprayed the air with antiseptics in our hospitals, but I doubt that any of us ever considered boiling *instruments and scrubbing our hands* as being terribly important."

At that moment Papa came slowly into the dining room. His cheeks had lost their ashen color and his gait, although labored, was steady.

"I thought I heard the doctor's voice," he said. "When are you going to check on your patient, young man?"

Wil pushed him gently into one of the chairs and felt his pulse. "I was just on my way to your bedroom, sir. Tell me, are you feeling better?"

A quick light leaped into Papa's eyes. "Better than I've felt in a long time. But I was afraid a good doctor like you would be back with Jonathan Letterman by now."

"I — " Wil Patten turned abruptly. "I won't be going back to the army. This — " he thrust out the still bandaged stub — "doesn't exactly permit it. But I've been of-fered a teaching fellowship in Georgetown University Medical School at the capital. I'll also be involved in research — perhaps on the need for antiseptics. Your daughter has tried to convince me my medical training hasn't been wasted after all. Those are the plans I've been working on this past week." He continued his examination silently.

"When will you leave?" Kirsten asked, her heart in her throat.

"As soon as — as I've completed my plans." He avoided her eyes, and she turned away, hurt and troubled.

I suppose once he returns to Washington, he won't come this way, she thought. But of course, she could never fit into his life anyhow.

Dr. Patten drew a bottle of powders from his kit. "Since you're doing well sir, I'll prescribe a lesser dosage of this medication. But please lie down now and rest until suppertime. It's time I'm on my way."

Papa struggled to his feet and reached for the doctor's arm. "God bless you, doctor. Our Lord has given you a great gift of healing, you know."

"Yes, I s'pose," Wil said with a wan smile. "But the best gift he gave me was his son, Jesus Christ. I first became aware of his love and grace when I visited your church more than a year ago, but it didn't make much sense to me then. When I learned that in Christ there's no North or South, and that he wants to work in the lives of those who will let him, I began to change my mind. This afternoon I stopped by the pathetically battered Dunker Church, and I saw how the shell had torn a hole through the very word I needed to claim — The Lord is *my* Shepherd. I knew my relationship to him was broken. It was only as I asked him to take over my life that this breach could be healed. He *is* my Shepherd now!"

He lowered his gaze and turned away, but Kirsten noticed the tears that glistened in the incredibly blue eyes, and her own grew moist.

Picking up his kit, he added, "I don't think I'll need to check on you again, sir, before leaving on my assignment," and with that he started for the door.

"Please come back — " Papa called weakly, but the young physician didn't turn.

Kirsten followed him, her heart full of joy and pain — joy, to know Wilshire Patten had found the God she served — and pain because he would soon go away and she would probably never see him again.

"Wil — " she began as she threw on her wrap and hurried after him. "Wil, I'm so happy. . . ."

He paused to tuck his kit into the saddlebag, avoiding her eyes. "I — it's hard to leave you, Kirsten, my darling. Once I thought maybe you and I — But — "

"Then don't go!"

"Oh, the spiritual barriers between us have been broken, but others remain."

"Yes," she nodded. "You are polished, wealthy, educated, and I'm a simple Dunker girl. . . ."

"No, no, that's not what I meant! My mother was deeply impressed with you. But

I can offer you *only one arm* — and you deserve better!" He placed one foot in the stirrup.

"No, Will!" she cried. "Please — please, why don't you ask me — what *I* want?"

"I must go, Kirsten." Swinging his lithe body into the saddle, he looked at her with a deep yearning glance, clucked to Beecher, and rode away without a backward look.

Kirsten watched him go, and a great heaviness swept over her. A pain that was as physical as it was emotional, wrenched through her. It was as though her life had suddenly come to an end. She had lived through so much these past months. How could she go through more anguish?

Slowly, woodenly, she walked toward the fence, and with hands that were numb she pushed herself between the rails. Her legs weighted like lead, she began to climb the hill. *I must catch one last look of him before he rides out of my life,* she thought.

The sun had slid below the horizon and the red glow at the rim of the world faded into pink, with saffron clouds cupping the distant hills beyond.

Quickly she whirled around and strained her eyes toward the east, to catch one final glimpse of a lone black stallion and its rider, making their way toward the pike. Yet horse and rider seemed to have vanished, and her heart wept.

Just then she heard a slight sound behind her, and with great effort she turned — and froze. Wil Patten was coming toward her, his thick brown hair riffling over his forehead in the evening breeze, the pucker between his eyebrows sharp and clear.

"Wil!" The word was a prayer as she started toward him. He walked slowly, as if forcing his way toward her, and she noticed his intense blue eyes held a questioning hope.

"Kirsten. . . ." He reached her in one giant step, and she found herself in his arms. Pushing back the creeping tendrils of her hair from her cheeks, he cupped her chin in the palm of his right hand. "I — I came back because I couldn't leave until I asked you — if this was only a foolish whim — or if you could really love half a man. I shouldn't have been so presumptuous. . . ."

"Oh, Wil — I do love you so!" she whispered, burying her head against his shoulder. "But our different backgrounds. . . . If it's my black bonnets and white net prayer caps — "

"We'll work that out. It's just that I can't offer you a whole — "

"How could you think only one hand

would make a difference when it's *you* I love?" Tears blurred her eyes as she lifted her face to his.

"Kirsten . . . when you didn't answer my letters, then came to me that bitter night last September for medical help, how could I think otherwise? That your interest in me was only as a doctor? And when I knew I could no longer live up to being even *that*. . . . Once you said your kisses were only a 'foolish whim.' I didn't want to believe you then, but — "

She placed her fingers against his lips. "Wil Patten, I've been foolish and arrogant. But I know that I love you and you love me, and we both have the Lord. That's all that really matters. You're right. We can work through the other barriers. My black bonnet is part of my church's tradition, a symbol of piety. But other churches also teach the Word."

She put her arms around him, felt his wide shoulders and the familiar hardness of his body. When he kissed her again, she gave him back kiss for kiss.

"I love you, Kirsten, and I'll never let you go," he said hoarsely. "Never again. . . ."

His lips were ardent, passionate, and they ripped away the shell she'd built around herself. Then, looking deeply into her eyes, he

261

caressed her face with the fingers of his right hand.

"When I've established a practice I'll come back and marry you. Will your family manage without you, do you think?"

She laughed softly. "The family will manage very nicely, now that Martin's here, and Lelo is finally ready to take my place, I think. I may be dependable, but never indispensable!"

"My mother will love that," he said whimsically. "She told me you were a girl with good common sense. She said I was a fool if I let you get away."

He turned his head toward the west. "Look!" he cried. "We can see the Potomac from here. With God, our life can be as bright as that splendid vista before us."

Together they watched the darkening valley, the gleaming sunset on the pewter-tinted river, and the silvery mist iridescent on the opposite bluff as the scene unfolded like a majestic panorama. The moment was golden, as would be the rest of their days together.